Filled Potential

Lainey Davis

Filled Potential:
Stag Brothers Book Two

By Lainey Davis

© 2018 Lainey Davis

Want to keep up with Lainey's new releases?
Sign up for my newsletter for a free story, exclusive content, and more!
laineydavis.com

Many thanks to Nicky Lewis, Doodle , and Keith G for editorial input.

Thank you for supporting
independent authors!

CHAPTER ONE
Juniper

There's nothing like the pull of the oars on the river at sunrise. I'll never grow tired of this feeling, alone in the water, just me and the current. I was a girl on fire this morning. I pulled out a 10k in record time. Probably because I'm so excited about my job offer. I was fairly certain I'd get offered a position at the firm where I interned my last year of law school, but nothing is ever certain until the ink is dry on the contract.

I feel so proud of myself as I slip back into my sandals on the dock before hoisting my boat above my head, carrying it back into the spot I rent in the boathouse. I pay more to house my beloved scull than I pay Zack for rent. I don't feel too badly about that, though, because his parents have been paying the lease on our apartment for years.

I wonder for the thousandth time why I'm still with Zack. As I walk toward home, I hear my father's concerned voice. *Juniper Jones, I didn't raise you to settle.* All through college, Zack was just...safe. Between my training for crew and trying to graduate early, I didn't have much time to devote to relationships. I fell into an easy rhythm with Zack. He was a year older than me, but we graduated at the same time and moved in together into the apartment along the Charles a few blocks from his father's investment company where Zack now works.

As I walk home, I think about how I've been wanting to move. Somewhere maybe closer to my new office. We could find a middle ground, a place that's really just ours, now that I won't be living off student loans. My mind is adrift with possibility as I mount the stairs to our townhouse on Sparks Street. A light in the front room is on, which registers as strange this early in the morning, but I throw my keys on the table and head upstairs. I'm quiet so I don't wake Zack. He's not a morning person. Stopping in the bathroom to turn on the shower to warm up, I walk toward

1

our room and strip out of my sweaty clothes, tossing them in the hamper.

I'm not sure what makes me look up, but I do. I look at our bed and see Zack sitting in it. Next to a naked woman with the covers pulled up to hide her breasts. Zack looks stunned. The woman sneers at me and says, "Are you planning to join us then?"

CHAPTER TWO
Ty

I stare at my name on the contract, watching as the black ink dries on the page. The background noise of the restaurant fades out as I look at the papers on the table. My brother Tim sits across from me, grinning from ear to ear. "Welcome home, little brother," he says, rising to fold me into a hug.

Well, he doesn't really *fold* around me. I'm probably twice the size of him now, and I remind him of this. "You can barely get your arms around me these days, dude." But not even a tradition of goofing around can overpower the emotions I'm feeling right now.

After years playing with the Vancouver Blades and then festering back in the minors, I've been signed by Pittsburgh. Hockey has taken me all over the world and now, finally, it's bringing me back home. This time with a hefty raise and a multi-million dollar, air-tight NHL contract. My brother represents the players' union and worked with my agent to fine-tune my contract. My agent Matty, the execs from the Fury, and Tim all took me up on Mt. Washington to sign my contract with their idea of a celebration dinner: fine dining with a sprawling view of the city from the glass windows of Le Monte. "I can't thank you enough for this, Timber," I say, looking into his eyes.

Tim's looked out for me and my brother Thatcher ever since our mom died in a car accident when I was 9. Our dad never got over it and has basically been drunk ever since. Tim took over as our parent. Enforced our curfew, made sure we kept our grades up. All that shit. Now he's making sure I'm treated right, and I'm grateful to him.

I shake hands with the suits from the Pittsburgh Fury before they head out, leaving me with my agent and my brother and our rare steaks.

Matty, my agent, starts talking about arrangements. I got called up pretty late in the season, but career ending injuries for other guys mean life-changing opportunities for me. As my brother reminds me, this is my chance to get my shit together, rein in my temper, and play some fucking hockey. The Fury are in the Stanley Cup playoffs and my contract has me starting practices this coming Monday. I haven't even moved my shit out of my apartment in Canada yet. I'm getting bored already with this meeting. I want to really celebrate. I nod along as Matty explains how he'll send in some professional movers to pack up my personal shit and ship it over here. I'll have to get all new Fury-branded gear anyway, so I don't need much more than the Armani suit I'm wearing. "Matty," I say, clapping my hand on his shoulder. "I'm 100% certain you'll take care of everything and whatever you miss, my brother here will clean up." I stand up. I need to get out of this place, to celebrate and live a little. "If you'll excuse me, I believe I'm going to find some fans."

I slip off my tie and jacket and hand them to my brother. He shakes his head as I walk out of the fancy-ass restaurant, shouting after me to "wrap it up, Ty! I'm serious!" My brother knows me well. There's only one thing I want on an evening like this, and that's a firm pair of tits in my face while I'm balls-deep in some pussy.

I walk along Liberty Ave until I find a club where the bouncer recognizes me and sends me inside with a nod. I slide up to the bar, order myself a top shelf tequila, and almost immediately, a smoking hot chick winds her way through the crowd, straight toward me.

CHAPTER THREE
Juniper

This is so unlike me. I don't wear short, tight dresses. I don't wear high heels; I don't go to nightclubs. I also don't move 600 miles with two days' notice, accept a job after a phone interview, or put french fries on my sandwiches. And yet, here I am. This is New Juniper. Pittsburgh Juniper. Doesn't-take-shit-or-tolerate-cheaters Juniper.

That morning I found Zack in bed with that woman, I threw on a bathrobe and walked right back out of the house--I didn't even stop for my shoes. One of my crew teammates, Lisa, lives close by the house I used to share with Zack and I crashed at her place while I made frenzied phone calls. She, as it turned out, has a brother who works for a law firm in Pittsburgh. They do sports law, had just landed a contract with the local NHL players union, and needed to bring on new attorneys pronto.

I had an interview with Tim Stag, the owner, over video chat. He offered me the job and actually smiled when I negotiated extra PTO instead of a higher salary than his initial offer. Like I explained to my Boston rowing team, I'll move just about anywhere that's got a river and a boathouse. But I'm not going to give up the regatta circuit and I need plenty of vacation time if I want to race with a women's team.

Lisa and her brother, my new colleague Ben, actually reached out to the rowing club in Pittsburgh for me. He doesn't row, but he knows from his sister that crew is a tight community. They hooked me up with a lead on a furnished apartment down the bike path from their boathouse. I didn't even go back to my townhouse to get anything. Fuck it. I can afford new clothes with the salary Stag is paying me. Everything I really cared about was already stored in the boathouse in Cambridge. I just packed it all up, strapped my boat to my roof rack, and drove to my new home without looking back.

For the first time in years I feel like I'm making the best decision for me. Not the safest. Not by a long shot. But this job feels like it's got growth potential and it felt good to walk away from that cheating slimeball.

There's only one thing left to do to cleanse myself of that entire experience with Zack: I need to fuck someone else.

Zack was my first and only so far. I'm 24 years old. I've always done everything just like I was supposed to do it. Stayed a virgin all through high school. Kept good grades all through undergrad and dated the first guy who asked me out after we met studying at the library. I didn't even sleep with him until we'd been together for a year. I realize now he probably only accepted that because he was probably fucking other women the entire time. Who the hell gets a booty call at 6 in the morning anyway? I try not to think about the logistics of him fucking someone else during my morning row.

Tomorrow, I'll meet my new rowing team and take out my frustrations on the Allegheny River. Tonight, I've decided to get laid. I probably could sleep with any number of guys from the boathouse. But that would get messy and complicated and I'd have to see them again almost daily. I want someone whose name I don't even know. Some cocky, attractive asshole who isn't interested in my number. Sex has never been that great for me anyhow, so I figure anyone will do. I just need for Zack's dirty dick not to be the last one that's been inside me.

I straighten out my too-short skirt, smooth down my short, inverted bob, and walk into the night club. I take a look around until I spot my target. Over by the bar stands a massive man who looks cocky enough that he won't want to talk to me again after tonight. He must be at least 6'3", without an ounce of fat on his firm body. I can see the muscles of his shoulders filling out his shirt and immediately want to run my fingers along his arms. I don't bother to look away when he sees me staring at him. He's got a messy crop of dark hair, but striking, grey eyes. The way his designer clothes hug his body tells me he appreciates nice things. He'll do just fine, I decide, and walk right up to him.

CHAPTER FOUR

Ty

This chick moves with absolute confidence. It's like she parts the crowd with her attitude. People seem to move out of her way as she glides straight toward me. I can tell from her toned, tan arms that she's in great shape. She's solid--not skinny, or fragile. I like a girl with meat on her bones, and this girl has it stacked in all the right places.

I sip my drink and watch her walk, noting her defined quads beneath a tight, black tank dress. When she stands in front of me, she's almost as tall as I am, which throws me a bit, because the women I fuck are usually so short it's hard for me to do them standing up. This chick is in heels, but I'd guess she's 5'10" in her bare feet. I run a hand through my hair and decide she will be just the right size for just about anything.

She holds eye contact with me as the bartender asks what she wants. Not moving those liquid brown eyes an inch, she says, "I'll take whatever he's having."

I give her my best smile, the one with two dimples, and tell the guy to stick it on my tab. This is going to be interesting. I raise my glass to her and say, "What should we drink to?"

She frowns, thinking about it, and says, "The Steel City and new adventures." We clink glasses and she downs the shot. No salt, no chaser. Just belts it down and doesn't even cough. She's used to good tequila I guess.

I realize that she's not here with anyone, which is unusual. Chicks usually move around in groups to ward off jerks like me who just want to fuck them. "You're here alone," I say, eyebrow raised.

"No," she says, signaling to the bar tender for another shot. "I'm here with you." And damned if that doesn't make me hard in an instant.

We spend another few minutes in a weird sort of silence that isn't quite awkward, but not quite comfortable, either. This chick doesn't do small talk. She also seems to have no idea who I am, which is unusual in a

7

club like this. A lot of the pro athletes in Pittsburgh come here to unwind. I can see a few football players surrounded by women on the dance floor and over on couches in the VIP area. Hell, a few of my new teammates nod at me as they head off to dark corners with a scantily clad woman on each arm.

"So," I start to ask, touching her arm. She doesn't bristle or move away, but she doesn't lean into me, either. "You wanna dance?"

She shakes her head and grabs my hand. "What I want is for you to take me someplace private and fuck me."

My eyes go wide and I look around. Is this chick for real? I mean, I'm totally down to fuck, but I don't usually get offers like that. I have to work a bit harder, even with the puck bunnies. Most of them want a little dancing first, at least. Some sort of pretense that we're not going to just go screw our brains out and then part ways. There's something really different about this girl, but I don't think she's drunk.

She doesn't seem high. "What gives, sweetheart? Are you for real?"

Her eyes flash and I can tell she's fired up about something. "I'm as real as they come. Now are you going to fuck me or should I find someone else to do the job?"

Hm, so she wants an angry fuck, I think. *Well, if it's got to be somebody, it might as well be me*, I decide. I pull her hand and walk toward the VIP bathrooms. I tip my chin toward the bouncer standing discreetly in the shadows as I push open the door. The bathrooms here are singles, each one a separate room with a door that locks. Habitual chivalry kicks in and I hold the door open for…shit, I don't even know her name.

She walks in ahead of me and as I close the door, she crashes against my chest. Her mouth is on fire against mine, pleading and desperate. I sink my teeth into her plump lower lip and I love the tortured little moan that escapes her throat. I twist the lock on the door and get to work with Jane Doe, sliding one hand along her ass and bringing the other slowly up to cup her tits.

Her body is firm and muscled. I love the feel of her against me, those thick thighs wrapped around my leg. She opens her eyes and I think I see a flicker of doubt, but then I start circling her nipple with my thumb and her face melts into pleasure. "You like that?" I keep my voice low and she nods as I tweak her nipple into a firm peak. I like watching this chick respond to my touch. I dip my head to suck on her breast, my tongue soaking the fabric of her thin dress. She thrusts her hips against me, her hands digging into my shoulders as I go to work on her chest.

God, even her tits are firm. *What the hell does this chick do to work out?* I shake my head a bit to resume focus and then move a hand down her chest, rubbing her pussy through her dress. Everything about her body is so firm, and I fucking love that, but what I really like is how she's so into this. She seemed really angry back at the bar, but I can tell she is as turned on right now as I am. I can feel the heat of her arousal, the damp cloth of her dress as I press my finger against her slit. I can hear her breathing fast as I begin to slowly, slowly circle her clit with my thumb, but I see in her eyes that her mind is wandering. No fucking way is she going to think about something else while she's fucking me. I'm going to be the only thing she can think about. I'm going to take over her mind as I make her body explode with pleasure. I move one hand to lift her skirt. I slide a hand between those hot thighs that she spreads wide, straddling my leg. My fingers reach her slit and--"Holy fuck, baby. No panties?"

She looks me in the eye again, those dark eyes almost black, her pupils are so dilated. She slides her hand down my chest toward my cock and says, "I told you. I came here to fuck." She struggles with my belt, trying to get my pants down in a hurry.

"Easy now, beautiful." I take her wrists in one hand and spin us so she's pressed against the white tile wall. "See that mirror over my shoulder?" She nods and I start to stroke her clit. She is sopping wet, slick with arousal. "I want you to watch yourself come on my hand, and then you're going to come on my cock." I slip a finger inside her, then another. She's into it, and it's making me very, very hard as I pump my hand in and out of her body. But soon I feel her attention drift again. Fuck that. When her eyes lose focus again I kiss her, pulling back to say, "Eyes on me, then. I'm going to watch you come."

CHAPTER FIVE

Juniper

What is he doing to me? Nobody has ever done anything like this to me before. As soon as my thoughts slip away to Zack and how his pitiful ministrations were nothing compared to this, my Romeo grabs my chin and forces me to look him in the eye while he fucks me with his fingers.

He's got my wrists pinned above my head against the wall and I'm totally at his mercy here. And I fucking love it. He's taking charge of this entire situation, so confident. Everything he's doing feels like a custom move designed to drive me wild. He is literally stirring my body into a frenzy with his long, thick fingers. God, if his fingers feel like this, what will his dick be like? Zack always fumbles around in his own rush to climax without much skill at getting me there, so I usually let my mind wander off. But this feels so good. I want to be here, in the moment. This is new to me. I never feel focused like this except when I'm rowing.

Mr. Huge, Dark, and Handsome bites my nipple and I scream. And then he grins this devilish, crooked smile as he slides another finger inside my body. My breath catches and my heart is racing as the pad of his thumb finds some secret rhythm against my clit I didn't know I needed. I'm getting so wet while he touches me. I can feel his hand getting slick with my wanting, and I feel my bones melting away, my legs shaking as something bursts inside me. As I stare deep into his grey eyes, he makes something explode. Something I've never felt before this moment. Something so fucking good that I can't control the sounds escaping my mouth. "Holy shit," I yell.

Who the fuck is this guy and how does he know what to do with my body? This bar trip feels like the best decision I've made in *years.*

He growls and nips at my neck. "That's gorgeous, sweetheart. You're so fucking sexy, coming on my hand." My hips buck against his hand and waves of pleasure rip through my body. I am shameless, rolling my pelvis against him, desperate for more friction, more of everything. He has reached inside me and pulled this orgasm from somewhere deep, yanked it out of me while staring into my eyes. And I know once will never be enough. Except it has to be. This is just a one-time thing to help me forget.

My chest heaves as I gasp for breath. He lets go of my wrists and my arms sink to my sides. I don't notice him unzipping his pants, but from somewhere in my consciousness I hear him rip open a foil packet. He leans close to my ear, whispering, "Are you ready for the next one? Cuz that was just the beginning."

When I open my eyes and look down, I laugh out loud--a single, snorting huff of incredulity. Surely the massive piece of granite in his hand isn't real? "There's no way that fucking thing will fit inside me," I breathe.

His wolfish smile returns and he strokes his giant dick while he massages my thigh with his other hand. "I'm pretty excited to give it a try, babe." He nudges my legs wider and I keep my eyes locked on his as I feel the tip of him pressing against my entrance. I hold my breath as he starts to work his way inside. I'm surprised to realize how much I am looking forward to this. Whatever the hell just happened with his hand, I know his cock is going to bring a new level of heat. He slides inside me slowly, letting my body adjust to his size. And I feel so full, like he's invading every spare inch inside me.

He smiles as he inches deeper and I exhale, feeling myself stretch to accommodate him. "Look down," he says, and I do. I look between our bodies, past the bunched up material of my dress, to see myself fully seated against him, my body pressed against the dark hair of his crotch. And then he starts to move.

Suddenly everything my teammates ever giggled about makes sense. He's got his rock-hard arms wrapped around me, holding me tight against his massive chest while he fucks me, and I'm enveloped in the smell of him, the warm feel of him. Everything smells like pine and mint and tequila. God, I want to see what he has under his suit. I fist his shirt as the pleasure starts to build. My head falls back, and he nips at my throat with his straight, white teeth. My body craves what he is doing, and more. "More," I whisper, and he looks at me with those grey eyes. "Harder," I say, not knowing how I know that's what I need. But he complies, fucking me so that my hips slam against the wall, my ass bouncing from the tile. When I look over his shoulder into the mirror, it's just as he said it would be. I see his hips pistoning into my body and I see my face transformed by pleasure.

And then he slides a hand between our bodies, rubbing his giant thumb knuckle so gently against my needy bud, and I rocket over the top again. I hear myself screaming as my hips thrash against him. I pound my fists against his chest, forgetting myself, and then I bury my face into his neck. I start to suck on his earlobe, run my fingers through his tousled hair, feeling the sweat build along his neck as he works my body. "Yes," he grunts, moving faster and faster. "Fuck, that's so good. Holy fuck, baby." And then he stills as I feel his cock throbbing inside me.

I'm slick with sweat and weak from the exertion of the most intense orgasms I've ever experienced. I heave against the wall, feeling like I just raced a regatta. I slide over a bit, seeking the cool tile behind my back. "That was--"

He kisses me then, a different sort of kiss. Long and deep, sensual. Personal. "That was incredible," he says, and winks.

He walks over to the trash to throw out the condom and starts washing his hands. I stare at him in the mirror above the sink, marveling at his half-hard dick. "I can't believe that thing fit inside me," I say, adjusting my skirt.

He grins and hands me a paper towel. "You know, I never do get tired of hearing that." I wash my hands and dab cool water on my neck, smoothing out my hair while he tucks himself back in. I'm not sure what comes next, because I fulfilled my mission here, but it wasn't at all what I expected. He reaches for my hand, his thumb gently stroking my wrist. The thumb he just used to get me off. "So can I get your name at least? Maybe your number?"

I sigh, letting out a long breath. *Shit.* "Sorry," I say, pulling back my hand. "That's not how this works." And, before I can change my mind, I open the door and march out of the bathroom, out of the club, into a cab toward home.

CHAPTER SIX
Juniper

The next morning I feel sore, but I don't mind. It's the kind of slight ache that makes me smile, remembering how good it felt with that guy in the bathroom. So now I know what passion feels like. Passion for a person, anyway. I've always felt a similar thrill from my sport. Ok, not quite similar. Sure, winning feels good. Whatever the hell that was last night? That felt like lightning struck and jolted me awake. I don't ever want to go back to sex the way it used to be.

But I do miss the water. It's been days since I last rowed! I feel off kilter without the water. I need to visit my scull at the boathouse, make sure she made the trip safely. I drag my sore body out of bed, get dressed, and walk the few short blocks to the boathouse for my first row in my new city.

My boat looks just beautiful, and I'm relieved to see she made the trip just fine. I carry her down to the dock, checking her out, re-assembling my oar locks, when the women's team heads down the ramp carrying their 8-seater propped on their shoulders. Once their boat's in the water, I introduce myself.

One thing I love about rowing is that the community is so friendly. There's not a bit of awkwardness as they welcome me to Pittsburgh. I even meet their coach, Derrick, and find out the details about practices for the women's team. Before they shove off, they invite me to go out for breakfast with them after practice, and so I spend an hour anticipating the easy conversation among like-minded new friends.

My oars dip into the brown water of the channel between the island and the north bank of the river, and I head up against the current. Once I set an easy pace, my mind drifts back to last night. *What the hell was that,* I wonder again. If that's how sex is supposed to feel, I decide I'm really angry with myself for settling with Zack for so long. *Four fucking years,* I grunt, digging in with my thighs and rowing faster as I think about him.

How could I not know? How could I be so focused on my career, so in tune with my surroundings on the water, but not know the man who said he loved me was playing me for a fool? I reach the dam on the river much faster than I anticipated. I pull toward the side and catch my breath. I see the women's team boat working on their race start technique. Every oar is in perfect unison. All their legs move together. Hell, I know even their breath is connected. They are a unit, a team. They help each other. That's what I need to focus on. Work and rowing. Everything else just winds up a disappointment.

The team meets at a diner nearby after their practice. Derrick claps me on the back and asks about rowing in Boston. He winks and asks me what the men looked like on my team there, and I relax all the more. I'm definitely not in the mood to think about dating anyone, especially after what happened last night, so knowing the male coach doesn't play for that team takes some of the pressure off.

When the table asks me if I've met anyone here, I can't control my blush, but it does feel good to say I had a good time at a club last night. I leave the diner with all their cell numbers, plans to go for a run over my lunch break later this week, and 9 new friends pestering me for more info about my tryst.

"It was just a bar hookup, guys," I say, downing the rest of my cranberry juice.

Tina, the coxswain, laughs. "Well, you'll have to come out with us next weekend and help me find a bar hookup who makes me blush like that."

~~~~

Monday morning I meet Ben for coffee before heading into my new office. The area around our building is all cobblestone streets and plate glass buildings. There's a cute little sitting area in the middle of the square, where I'm surprised to see Ben sitting at a two-top with a flat white for me. He grins. "My sister told me your drink." I sink into the chair feeling very welcome in this new city and, for the thousandth time, grateful that I have the rowing community to support me in so many ways. "Lisa told me I'm supposed to say they're useless without you, and you'd better return her call or she's going to come hit you over the head with an oar."

That's Lisa. I make a mental note to call her after work today, tell her about my new job once I get a sense of the place.

"Thank you so much for everything, truly," I tell him. "I'm so glad to finally meet you in real life and not just on FaceTime with your sister! Your whole family really saved my ass."

Ben waves his hand at my thanks. "So," he says, "You ready

for what's up there?"

I shake my head. "No! I have no fucking clue what to expect, actually. Tell me everything." Ben describes Stag Law, how in just four years it grew into a multimillion dollar firm under Tim Stag's calculated direction.

"The man is serious as hell, but it's actually a great place to work." The company represents the players unions for the professional football, baseball, *and* hockey teams in Pittsburgh, and so the majority of the work relates to contract negotiations, but there's a fair bit of injury work, termination disputes, and, as Ben explains, a lot of the athletes struggle to keep it in their pants. "We do a *lot* of paternity-custody cases…and then some defense work if they're caught with hookers and blow."

I'm not quite sure how I fit into this high-stakes, masculine world, but Ben explains that Tim really wants to build diversity on his staff. "That starts with you, I guess."

"Wait. I'm the only female attorney? I don't want to be here just to be the diversity."

He shrugs. "Like I said, the business is only four years old. Most of us have only been on staff for two years. I do know Tim was way interested in your resume and talked about you at the staff meeting after your interview. I think you're the only athlete as well. I mean, the rest of us work out. When we have time. But you are involved in team sports. Tim mentioned that your perspective would be really invaluable."

I nod and finish my drink. We walk upstairs and I'm introduced to the executive assistant, Donna. Ben tells me she is the one who really steers the ship. He whispers, "Donna knows everything about everything that happens here. Tim is totally fucked without her." *Noted: suck up to Donna,* I think as I shake her hand and give her my best smile.

"Juniper, you let me know if you need help with anything while you're getting settled," she says, squeezing my arm. I like her. I can tell her offer is genuine.

We walk into the corner office, a huge space with 2 walls of windows and a massive desk. Seated behind it is Tim Stag, looking impeccable and handsome in a tailored suit. He smiles to greet us, but I notice his smile doesn't quite reach his eyes. There's something familiar about him, but I can't place it. I decide I must just be recognizing him from my video chat interview. "Juniper Jones," he says, pumping my hand. "We meet at last. I hope Ben was filling you in about Stag Law?"

"I only told her the bad stuff," Ben jokes. Ugh. Male posturing.

We all laugh and at a nod from Tim, Ben ducks off to his own office.

Tim goes through his whole spiel again, even asking me about rowing because he seems really interested in this athletic perspective I bring to his team. "I've never had someone negotiate for time off versus increased salary," he says, and I smile.

"I take rowing as seriously as I take my work, Mr. Stag. I'm fast and efficient at both, but I need a lot of Fridays off to travel to competitive regattas."

"As you know, most of our clients are professional athletes," he says, and I nod. "One reason I was eager to hire someone with a team sport background is because I need my employees to understand our clients, but not get starstruck. You're going to be brushing shoulders with a *lot* of famous men, Ms. Jones. I take it you can keep your wits about you?"

This makes me laugh, since I don't really follow sports much outside of rowing. I practically grew up on the water. My dad was an Olympic rower and coached my team in high school. There was no room at the Jones household for drooling over football stars. "I promise to treat our clients like I would anyone else with a strict training regimen," I say. "I'd rather ask them about their anaerobic workouts than their prowess on the field."

Tim seems really pleased with this information and leans to grab a file. "Come on," he says, "Let me show you to your office and tell you about your first client." He walks me into an office a few doors down from his own. We're on the top two floors of one of the skyscrapers downtown, and from my window I have a great view of the confluence of the rivers. I feel a warm sense of anticipation, looking forward to mornings spent out there, days spent in here.

I run my fingers along the polished wood desk. A brand new laptop and extra monitor are angled away from the glare of the window. I vaguely pay attention as Tim tells me someone from IT will be in to get me set up with email and the company wifi.

I hang my bag on a hook and look at him, expectantly.

"May I sit, Juniper? Should I call you Juniper? We mostly do first names here, including clients, but stick with formal titles when pro executives are in..."

"Please sit," I say, sinking into my own leather desk chair, "And absolutely, call me Juniper." I adjust the levers on the side of the seat to accommodate my height and find that it hugs my body perfectly. I'm going to really love it here.

"I'm assigning you to my brother Ty, who plays for the Pittsburgh Fury as of this weekend," he says, and I feel my jaw drop.

"Your *brother* will be my first client? Tim, are you sure that--"

He cuts me off. "I want to review the details of my brother's contract negotiations before he comes in to meet you in a bit. I would

16

ordinarily handle this sort of case myself, but it's a conflict of interest. Him being my brother and all." I nod, and Tim tells me about Ty's transfer from Vancouver. The only thing unusual about the contract is that the Pittsburgh team, the Fury, are in Stanley Cup playoffs and Ty will immediately begin practices. We still need to work out the details of his playoff bonus.

"This seems relatively straightforward," I say to my boss, and I furrow my brow, still trying to place why he seems so familiar to me. "What's with the emphasis on morality and sportsmanship?" Tim coughs.

His face shifts, as he explains that his brother is a hot head who gets himself in trouble for fighting on the ice, and partying off the ice. *Great* I think. *A cocky, impulsive asshole.* Apparently this guy was on timeout in the minor leagues for a while and is getting his shot at redemption because a Fury player tore his ACL right before playoffs.

Tim's phone beeps several times and he stands. "I'll leave you to look it over, and I'll meet you in the conference room in an hour. Ty will be there along with his agent to look over paperwork." I nod as he backs out of the office, taking a call.

When I make my way to the conference room, I feel totally familiar with Tyrion Stag's Pittsburgh Fury contract. Shoulders back, confident, I push open the door ready to impress, and I freeze in my tracks. The blood drains from my face and I have to clutch the doorknob to steady myself. Sitting at the table with my new boss is *him*. The man from the nightclub. The guy I fucked last weekend is my client and, worse, my boss's brother.

CHAPTER SEVEN

Ty

"There she is!" My brother stands and walks toward the door and I look up. *Holy shit, it's her!* The woman from the nightclub, the broad with the hot thighs and the strong need to angry fuck. What are the fucking chances that she works here with my brother? That she's my new fucking lawyer?

This is going to be fun. I can tell.

She looks like she's seen a ghost. Yeah, she's rattled to see me here. Tim puts an arm lightly on her shoulder and ushers her into the conference room. That grinds my gears a little. I don't want my brother touching this woman. "Juniper Jones, this is my brother, Ty Stag."

She stands stiffly beside him but doesn't speak, and I can tell he's annoyed. He thinks she's starstruck because I'm famous, but I knew she had no idea who I was the other night. Nah. She's spooked because she fucked her client and she has no idea what happens next.

"Juniper, huh?" I stand and walk over to her, sliding my hand into hers for a shake. Her arm twitches when my hand makes contact with her skin. "My brother says you're new to Pittsburgh, too."

She nods and sits. I can see her trying to gather her wits. She looks at me, sort of desperately, and clears her throat. I just give her my best smile until she stammers, "Yes, things worked out quite nicely. Your brother hired me just as I was looking to make a change." And then she just stares at me uncomfortably until Matty clears his throat.

"Ok, well, now that we're all here, Juniper, Tim said you've reviewed the contract. Again, that's really pretty straightforward, but while we have the team together I wanted to talk about our agency's plan to help bolster Ty's image."

She starts chugging a glass of water while Tim glares at her. God, I love making my stiff-ass brother uncomfortable almost as much as I like seeing this woman squirm. I lean back in my chair with my hands clasped behind my head. Because I can. I'm paying these people to put up with shit like this.

Matty frowns at me, but continues, "Our first idea is to get Ty connected with the community back here in Pittsburgh. It's been awhile since he's been home and we're always looking for new opportunities for outreach. An obvious idea is to get him involved with youth sports."

My brother shakes his finger. "No. Sorry, Matty, but I have to disagree with you there. I don't think it's wise to put Ty in front of a bunch of kids until we know for sure he can keep his nose clean. Ty, no offense, but your reputation precedes you."

"None taken, dickwad. What's your next idea?"

Tim smiles and points two index fingers at Juniper. "Juniper is an athlete. I've been thinking about your image ever since I interviewed her. Juniper, what you said about amateur athletes using paid time off to compete, really negotiating to build a life around your sport...that really stuck with me."

Matty looks interested in this line of thought. "What sort of athlete are you then, Juniper?"

She blushes. "I'm a rower." *Fuck yeah, you are,* I think, remembering her firm arms and chest. Those thighs...Jesus. "But I'm new here, so I don't really--"

Tim cuts her off. "I did some research. There are a lot of amateur *adult* sports organizations in our city, ranging from deck hockey to Gaelic football. But I liked what I saw about the rowers." Tim and Matty bow their head over a folder Tim extracts from his briefcase, talking about adaptive rowing for people with disabilities and sponsoring teams so the inner city high schools can afford to participate in rowing.

Matty strokes his chin and claps Tim on the back. "This is why I love partnering with you, man. This shit is great." Juniper just sits with her mouth hanging open. Matty continues. "We'll get Ty on board as a sponsor of the team to the tune of--Juniper, what does it cost for oars or life jackets or whatever?"

"Team boats cost tens of thousands of dollars," she says, and my face falls a little thinking of how much it's going to cost me to polish my reputation. "I think it could be appropriate if Ty were to finance some of the indoor training facility upgrades, though."

"Indoor! Perfect. He can keep showing up to events year-round. I love it. Ty, we're going to reach out to the coach and have you shadow a few practices, wave a flag at the start of a race, or whatever the hell you call it. Juniper, is it a race? Is there a flag?"

She opens her mouth to speak, but Matty cuts her off again. "When's the next team practice?"

Juniper looks like she's seriously regretting ever moving to this city, but her next words wipe the smile off my face pretty quickly. "The women's team practices tomorrow at 6am."

My brother and my agent share a long laugh about this and tell me to get my ass to the dock at 5:45. Matty stands and claps Tim on the back again. "Tim, have Juniper finish up the language regarding Ty's playoff bonus and get a courier to bring that contract to my office later. Ty, baby, good to have you on board." He practically waltzes out of the conference room, but sticks his head back in and points at me. "5:45, dude. Seriously,   do   not   fuck   this   up."

CHAPTER EIGHT
Juniper

"So you fucked your client?" Lisa laughs at me when I call and tell her about my arrival in Steel City.

"It's not funny, Lisa! I could lose my job. I have to tell my boss I can't take on this client. Ugh! But then I have to tell him why..."

"Could you say you just don't like the big guy?"

I sigh. "I don't think I can do that. I can't be burning through jobs because of men. Asshole men. I'm off men, Lisa. No more men for me."

She laughs again. "From what you described, I'd say it was worthwhile. Did you say you were limping afterward?"

I roll my eyes and we hang up. She texts me that she thinks everything will work out, but I'm not so certain.

I don't sleep well. When my alarm sounds at 5:30, I groan and consider not getting out of bed. But then I remember that my rowing practice, formerly my sanctuary, my holy place, is now pretty much an extension of my work. I have to meet Ty Stag on the docks and introduce him to the team. *I* *have barely even met the fucking team*, I mutter as I heat up my oatmeal and slip into my workout clothes.

I brush my teeth, grab my bag, and walk the half mile trail along the river to the boathouse. I'm not sure whether I'm furious or relieved to see Ty leaning against the wall. He looks like a movie star, with his tousled hair and slate grey eyes. He fills out his designer jeans, I'll give him that. I can't help but stare at his forearms and the bulging muscles beneath his t-shirt cuffs. I've always had a thing for forearms. But I can't think things like that. Not about my client. *Why does he have to be so damn good looking?*

He spots me and grins. "Juniper Jones, nice to see you again." He looks at his watch. "Think we have time for a quickie before your coach gets here?" Then the bastard winks at me.

"Listen, Stag, you are never to discuss that night again. You are my client. Do you want me to lose my *job??* It's bad enough you've invaded my personal space and affected my training. I wish I didn't have to ask you not to jeopardize my career as well."

He throws up his hands. "Easy there, tiger. I can behave. I promise. Look, I'm new here, too." I raise an eyebrow at him. "I mean, I grew up here, but I've been gone since high school. It's not like I have a ton of friends outside my brothers and my teammates."

"*These* are *my* teammates, Stag," I hiss at him. Understanding dawns on him, then, and to his credit he does stop clowning around. My coach, Derrick, emerges from the clubhouse and heads down the stairs with a few of the rowers behind him.

"Juniper Jones! Welcome, welcome, welcome, my new meat wagon." I hate that nickname for the center pair of rowers in an 8-seat boat. I'm tall and solid, and I always get placed in the middle of the boat where they need my strength.

But I'm not about to make a stink about it. I want my coach to like me!

"Guilty as charged, I guess." I shake his hand, and smile at the other rowers I met at breakfast the other day. I can see them all ogling Ty, and I remember that he's a big celebrity. Tina is shifting around uncomfortably and I can tell she wants to hug him or make out with him. Or both. I'm glad she refrains. Pittsburghers love their sports stars. Even these amateur athletes are fawning over Ty as Derrick makes small talk and everyone gets ready to get on the water. Derrick turns to Ty and explains how practice will go--we will inspect the boat, set it in the water, warm up, and then he's going to send us on a long row to the confluence of the city's 3 rivers.

Derrick and Ty will follow along in a motor boat with a megaphone, barking out instructions in Derrick's case, and hopefully Ty won't be a distraction or get in the way. Not that Derrick or anyone else resents his presence here. Oh no, everyone is pretty ecstatic to have a source of funding and a little publicity for our program...and a hot guy to stare at, I guess.

Derrick explains that Matty gave him a call and planned out a whole promotional strategy. "Any new commercials and stuff for the Fury that feature Ty will show him at our facilities, talking with our athletes, stuff like that! Plus we get a set of season tickets for next year." Derrick winks at me and says, "It was a lucky day for our team when Juniper Jones landed a job in Pittsburgh!"

I flush, really wishing I'd had a chance to prove myself to them before feeling like I bought my way on the team with my work connections. Derrick snaps into game mode then and tells us to head into the boat house. Ty watches, seemingly fascinated, as we carry the boat to the water. "Dude," he says to Derrick. "Shouldn't we help them carry that thing?"

Derrick just laughs as we ease the boat gently into the water and slide in the oars. Ty has no idea how strong we are, apparently. Derrick clues him in on some of the rowing commands and even lets Ty yell into the megaphone as we warm up. I can't help but look at him in the boat, muscled arms crossed. Firm jaw, piercing stare.

But then we set our pace, heading toward the fountain at Point Park, and all other thoughts slip away. It's just me and the oars, feeling the pull of the water. I match my pace to the other women and together we dig deep   and   set   the   boat   flying.

CHAPTER NINE
Ty

From where I'm sitting in the motorboat with Derrick, I'm impressed that these women work so hard for their sport and don't get paid for it. They're doing a lot of the same things we do at hockey practice, just for the hell of it. At six in the fucking morning.

My coffee is long gone, but I don't need caffeine to feel the thrill of watching Juniper row. I can't take my eyes off her, loving the determination on her beautiful face as much as the movement of her long muscles. "Why'd you call Juniper a meat wagon?" I ask Derrick, hoping he's not going to say something about her ass that will cause me to punch him in the face.

"What do you notice about her," he asks, not turning his eyes from the boat.

"I mean, that's a pretty loaded question," I shout back, not sure I like where he's going with this. I feel really possessive about this girl, now that I think about it. I know I shouldn't be, and that makes me want her even more. Especially now that I've had a taste.

Derrick rolls his eyes, though. "Juniper is tall and strong as hell," he says. "I stuck her in the 5th seat because she's got a long stroke. She's the biggest and most powerful woman in that boat."

"Didn't you just meet her, like, this week?" I wonder how he can tell all of this.

He doesn't answer, but the longer I watch, even I can tell what he means. We're about a mile from the confluence, and they're moving at a pretty good clip. Some of the other women are sweating, breathing hard. Their faces look strained. It's got to be one hell of a workout. We must be miles from where they started, and they're in this tiny boat.

I let my eyes settle on Juniper. I see the defined muscles in her thighs as she slides her seat back and the long muscles of her arms as she pulls the oars. I think back to how good she felt pressed against me, how I wondered what she did to get her body to look and feel that way. As I watch her move so gracefully, I feel myself getting hard and I want very much to do something about that. With her.

I move past thinking with my dick for a minute to really look at her as an athlete. Derrick calls for the team to pick up the pace--the tiny girl in the front of the boat they call the coxswain is really screaming at them now--and everyone else is struggling. I can tell they're hurting. Then I look at Juniper's face and I notice something. This is easy for her. *She's holding back,* I realize.

The boat reaches the tip of the Point and Derrick yells, "Hold water!" Immediately, the women raise their oars and rest, their chests heaving. Juniper is breathing easy, like this was barely strenuous.

"Hey, Derrick," I say. "My attorney doesn't quite look winded yet. What happens if Juniper really takes it to the max?"

He smiles at me, and I can tell he's glad I saw what he saw. "Ty, my new friend, I am really excited to find out."

He blows a whistle and they turn the boat around, crossing the river in front of the barges and booze cruise boats getting lined up for the baseball game later. Since the team is fighting the current, he takes it easy on them with the pace, but even still, I can tell everyone is spent when they finally climb out on the dock. They all high five each other and head for the showers, asking Juniper if she's got time for breakfast.

She shakes her head and gestures toward me. "I've got to get to work and finish a contract for this guy so he can play in the game this weekend." I ask the team to remind me of all their names and promise to remember them when I come out again Thursday. I would have a whole host of new phone numbers by now if I weren't trying to keep my nose clean, but I realize I don't want any of this random tail anyway. I want what I can't have. I watch her walk up the path, longing to squeeze her ass again.

CHAPTER TEN

Juniper

Wednesday morning, I make time for the worst part of my move. I have to go to the DMV and change my driver's license. Tina tipped me off that the downtown DMV is the worst one, so even though it's further from work, I go to the office in East Liberty. It's in the basement of a gorgeous old building with a glass dome, which I'm busy staring at when someone taps me on the shoulder.

"Do you mind moving? You're blocking the stairs." A shaggy head moves to block my view, and I groan. Of course it's Ty stag.

"What the hell are you doing here??" Ouch. My tone is harsher than I intended, but I'm rattled to see him out in public. "Are you following me?"

He shrugs. "I'm here same as you, babe. Gotta get my PA license. In case you forgot, I've been living in Canadia, the hinterland, driving a bobsled and all that." I wish I weren't staring at his dimple when he smiles after joking around.

"Look, Ty, you *cannot* call me babe. Ever." He shrugs. I sigh and huff down the stairs to get in line. Of course there's a line. I can smell him when he stands a bit too close to me. He's got a hint of cologne today, something like pine with a citrus scent behind it. So subtle. Maybe it's aftershave. I try not to be obvious as I sniff him behind me. *What am I doing??*

"So hey," he says. I turn sideways, keeping my eye on the line of people, half looking at Ty. "I just wanted to...is thank you the right phrase for this? Anyway, I am really glad I got to see all that at the docks and on the river. I learned a lot."

I have no idea what he means, and I furrow my brow. He keeps talking. "Rowing seems really fucking intense. Can I ask you something? I noticed you weren't even tired from that training, and the rest

26

of them were talking about how their legs feel like jelly."

"Okay…"

"It reminded me of the other night. You know, in the bathroom?"

"Oh my god. No. Ty, just no. We are not discussing that." I turn around. Can this line move any slower? He reaches for my arm. I hate my traitorous body for feeling a spark from his touch. "Juniper, wait." I sigh and turn to look at him again. He runs his hand through his hair like he's not really sure where he's going with this. "I just…why do you hold back?"

"What did you say to me?"

"I said why do you hold back? During sex, while you're rowing…you had more in your tank…"

I can't move. I'm shaking with emotions I can't quite identify, but I need to make sure I heard him correctly. "Are you seriously talking about my sexual performance in relation to my rowing?"

"I mean, I know you were pissed off that night and it took awhile to get you to let loose while we were fucking, but I was just wondering what it takes to really open you up on the water…"

I don't even think about what happens next. I shove him as hard as I can, pressing both hands flat against his chest. Since he wasn't expecting the onslaught, he goes flying backwards, catching his head against the railing, nearly falling down the stairs. Once he regains his feet, he crumples, bent in half at the waist, moaning. "Jesus Christ, Juniper! What the fuck was that for?"

Shit. A security guard approaches. Fuck.

"Sir, is everything all right?"

Ty is doubled over, breathing heavy. He stands up and his nose is bleeding. "I'm fine. It's fine. I just tripped over my shoelace."

The security guard reaches for his radio. "We've got a situation here, Brad."

"Sir, really, I'm his lawyer. This is fine."

He raises an eyebrow at me. "You're going to have to come with me, ma'am."

Another security guard comes running up. Apparently this is Brad, and, now that Ty has wiped the blood off his face with his t-shirt, Brad evidently recognizes him. "Holy shit! This is Ty Stag! Yo, Ty Stag just got hit by some chick!"

The color drains from my face as I remember the morality clause in Ty's contract. He glares at me as a crowd begins to form. But then I see him enter PR mode, and I can tell he's been in this world for a long time.

"Brad, is it? Hey man, you wanna take a selfie with me?" Brad is beside himself, putting an arm around Ty, not caring about the blood staining his shirt. I rummage in my purse to see if I can find some tissues or something, but before I can hand anything to Ty, a woman wearing a hockey sweater comes out from the reception desk, shaking one of those ice packs from a first aid kit. *Of course, the Pittsburgh DMV staff are all hockey fans.*

Soon, he's signing autographs and joking with the staff about whether he looks more authentic for his driver's license with a swollen, red face. "What do you think, gals," he asks the room. "Should I pull out my fake teeth for the picture?" He waits a beat. "That's a joke. These are all real, ladies." They're eating it up. Even the DMV employees are smiling. I decide to slink away, out into the parking lot.

I don't slow down until I'm inside my apartment. I slam and lock the door behind me and turn the hot water all the way up in the shower. While I stand there letting it scald my skin, scrubbing Ty's blood from my arm, I feel myself about to cry. I shake my head, choking back my tears. I'm furious. I'm angry at Zack and angry to have moved here, and above it all, I'm angry at Ty Stag and I'm not even totally sure I know why.

If I'm honest, he's right about the rowing. I'm not tired after team training and that wasn't the hardest I've ever worked out, but what kind of showboat shows up and lets everyone know she's in better shape? I hear my dad again, talking to me about never settling. This isn't the same thing as settling for Zack. But god, Ty was right about the bathroom. I wasn't so much holding back as...shit. I had no idea sex could even be *like* that. The feelings he pulled from my body! I've never felt anything even close. I remember how he looked into my eyes, how his big hands felt on my body, but I can't go there right now.

I have to go to work...and he's my *client.*

Besides, neither Ty nor my dad ever had to know what it feels like to be different and stand out.

It's one thing being a tall woman. I can deal with that, and I don't even slouch like some of the other tall women I know who try to mask their height. Hell no. I wear heels and proudly. But otherwise? Where I grew up...if you stood out you got hurt. Rowing in a team gave me safety, support. Any time I've stood out, alone, that's when you get noticed.

Rowing crew, the whole goal is uniformity. Even if you've got the ability to go faster you need to match pace with your teammates. It's always worked well for me. I'm strong as the powerhouse, and they need me!

I finish my shower and get dressed for work, thinking about how I can possibly convince my boss to move his brother to another lawyer in the firm. Maybe that will be easier now that I punched a Stag in the face? This just isn't going to work well for me.

I text Lisa. ***Emergency. Can you talk?***

My phone rings an instant later, and I don't even say hello. "I shoved Ty at the DMV and he fell and got a bloody nose."

"Say what now?"

I relay most of the story to Lisa, saying only that he said something rude and I wasn't thinking.

"Hang on a sec." I hear a rustling in the background, a clicking sound. "Oh shit. June, go to your laptop."

"What? Why?"

"Just pull up TMZ."

It takes a minute to load, but I see a gossip story about Ty, bloody and grinning with the staff at the East Liberty DMV. "Mother fucker."

Lisa is reading aloud. "Pittsburgh hockey hottie gets the hand when he hits on a hometown gal. That's not a bad headline," she says. "It looks like they're making it sound fun. Ty must be really good with the public. Look how even the guard is excited to hug his bloody ass."

"What do I do, Lees?"

There's a long pause and I can tell she's reading and searching the web for more news. "I think you ignore it. Or maybe, like, apologize to him? Send him a bottle of aspirin?"

"You are useless." I shove my feet in my heels and grab my bag.

"At least I'm not guilty of assault! Go take it out on the water later."

I sigh. It's going to be a long day at work.

When I arrive, I grab Tim by the break room for a word. He is more animated than I've seen him so far. He is evidently thrilled with the contract work I've done so far for his brother, loves the campaign to clean up Ty's image, and says Matty called about some good press on the gossip columns.

"Good press?"

Tim grins. "My brother was working the fans. I think he got fresh with some feisty woman and she gave him a bloody nose. I don't know. Matty says it looks great from his perspective. Ty really has matured. A few years ago, this would have been a sex scandal story." My jaw hangs open, and Tim says he wants me to meet with him later about taking on some of the MLB players to my client portfolio.

I sigh and sink into my desk. What is it about this city? Nothing makes sense here. I lose myself in my work, preparing contracts for everyone Tim suggested, and I don't come up for air until well past dark.

CHAPTER ELEVEN

Ty

When I show up to practice with a black eye, coach looks at me like he wants to punch me in the other one. I tell him I was horsing around with my brothers, but I can tell he's not buying it.

"You don't think my people tell me about the gossip, Stag? I fucking read the Internet. What did we talk about? No fights. No chasing tail."

"No, sir." I shake my head, but he puts a meaty hand on my chest.

"Lace up and get out on the ice. Make me happy I signed you."

Great. What the fuck got into Juniper? I mean, yeah, I said something sorta rude, but I wasn't expecting her to check me like that. Hell, she'd give some of these guys a run for their starting spot. I should bring her to practice sometime. I wonder how hot she'd look in hockey pads?

I manage to forget about it and get in a good practice, but while I'm getting iced down later, I decide to call Juniper on her little jab. She picks up after one ring.

"Ty."

"You trying to get *me* fired so you're not my lawyer anymore so I'll fuck you again, baby?"

"I swear to Christ, I'm not even sorry anymore, Ty."

"Easy, easy. I just called you to let you apologize. I'm in an ice bath right now, so I've got time to wait for you to gather up all the humble pie you want to eat."

I hear her snort, but I'm not going to let her off easy. "My face hurts so bad, Ju-jo. I'm worried I will have to get PT. You might have cracked my orbital bone."

"All right, all right. Ty. I am sincerely sorry that I shoved you and that is never ok, no matter what awful thing you said to me."

I settle deeper into the whirlpool tub. This shit feels so good on my aching body, and the sound of Juniper's voice in my ear feels good in a different way. "How are you going to make it up to me?"

"Excuse me?"

"The whole Internet knows I got rejected by an angry girl. They think I'm some scoundrel now. I'm probably going to get a lot of panties thrown at me on the ice."

"Well, then I guess I helped your dating prowess, so that's how I'll make it up to you."

"I'll think of something, Juniper Jones."

She snorts again. I love all these noises she makes. "See you on the dock tomorrow morning?"

"Yes, Ty, I'll see you on the dock."

Again, I watch with Derrick from the motorboat while the team rows. Again, I stare at Juniper the whole time. I ask Derrick some questions about her form, what he looks for when he's coaching. He talks about breath and unity. Everything he says, I see Juniper doing perfectly. Perfectly. She makes me think back on how hockey was for me in junior high. I was so much better than everyone around me, it really stalled my own progress until Tim got me transferred into a different school with a better hockey program. That's when my career really took off. I wonder if Juniper's rowing team in Boston was better than this one, but when I Google it, they seem about evenly matched.

I look at Derrick and wonder if he's the Tim she needs to kickstart her rowing.

On the ice, everything is going so great. I gel with my teammates. I remember some of these guys from junior leagues and we've played against each other before. It's not like we're strangers. I'm starting to get a feel for their pace and energy, but of course you can never really tell until you're in a game with these guys.

I'm ready for a game.

Sunday arrives and I fucking love the butterflies in my stomach. This all just feels so right and so surreal at once. As I'm lacing up, some of the guys pound me on the shoulder. I look down at my gear, stare at my name STAG on a Pittsburgh jersey.

My whole life, I've dreamed of playing with the Fury. My hometown team. Today is the day.

I know my brothers and my grandma are up in the suite above center ice. I am pretty sure Juniper is up there, too. I want her to see me play, and I realize I really want her to be impressed with me as an athlete. That's weird for me. I really never give a shit what women think about me. I mean, most of the ones I sleep with are mostly with me because I'm famous and I have a nice body. That's just plain objective fact. But none of them ever know anything about me as a person. About what it means to be good at a sport like this.

As they announce my name, I skate a lap around the ice, and I feel so grateful. I remember everything about why I play this sport, why I worked so hard my whole life to be out here.

At the face off, some guy from Colorado starts saying some shit to me, but who gives a fuck? "Hear you got beat up by a chick, Stag." What do I care what this asshole thinks? Halfway into the first period, I slam him into the boards, steal the puck from him, and pass to my guy Kingston, who shoots it right into the corner of the net. Fucking swish. That's what I'm talking about. I don't even feel like I need to fight. What the hell was I so angry about playing before, anyway? Scoring against these assholes feels way better than fighting with them.

All game long, the Colorado guys are trying to bait me, and what do I do? I look over at Coach, and I score two fucking goals, that's what I do. In a playoff game. Everything clicks, I can see where my teammates are going to be, and I connect with them. When we change lines, Coach claps me once on the back and pounds my helmet. Yeah. I'm good here.

I barely recognize myself now, though, getting back pats in the locker room, joking around. When they moved me to the minors to get my shit together, I just felt like that pissed me off more. Hell, I got in more fights playing minor league hockey and spent more time in the sin bin than I ever did in the big leagues.

But I don't know. Sometime in the past year, I got sick of all that shit. I guess maybe I grew up. I'm still a cocky asshole. But damn if it doesn't feel better to win the game than it does to win the fist fight.

The press is waiting outside the locker room, and I decide to talk to them before I shower. I know my eye is still black and blue, but half these guys are bloody and bruised after the game. I know they're going to ask me what changed out on the ice. "The truth is, I'm really glad to be back in my hometown," I tell the guy from ESPN. "Lacing up for the Fury today, with my brothers in the stands, was really a lifelong dream for me."

"Ty, how were you able to keep your temper in check today? That's been an issue for you since you started your pro career."

I work hard not to roll my eyes at this guy. "I started pro when I was still a teenager, right from high school. I've come a long way since then. You know, my coaches here have a strong game plan. My teammates and I play for each other. It's easy to keep my eye on the goal and tune out all the background noise." *That'll shut him up, right?* I can see my coach nodding and Matty gives me a thumbs up.

As the press slowly files out, the other guys talk about how they're going to celebrate. I consider ditching my plans with my brothers to join the guys at the strip club, but I realize that I just don't feel like doing that. The only set of cans I'm interested in seeing was up in the suite with my family today, and I can't exactly go call her up for a celebration fuck. And I hate that.

Who have I become that I'm more excited to go sign my contract update tomorrow than I am about winning the most important hockey game I've ever played? I roll into my house before 11pm, and even my grandma is surprised to see me.

"Tyrion Stag," she yells from her bedroom. "I didn't expect you to come home tonight!"

I sit on the edge of her bed, still wearing my suit and tie. Our coach insists on "number ones" for all the official business after the game. I know I look damn good. Gram acts like she's picking a piece of fuzz off my shoulder, but I think she just wants an excuse to pat my arm. "I'm so glad to have you back home, you know," she says. "It was good to watch you out there, to watch your brothers enjoying you play."

She smiles at me and I pull her close. Gram has basically been the only mother in my life. I was really young when my mom died, not even ten years old. Dad never recovered and drank himself into…"Hey, Gram," I ask her. "Do you even know where Dad is these days?"

She sighs and sits back against her pillows. "I haven't heard from or seen him in months. He's still around…somewhere." She clutches at the locket around her neck, where she's got a picture of the 6 of us. Mom, Dad, Gram and her 3 grandsons. A happy family from a long time ago, who've been scattered for a long time. "I bet he watched your game though, from whatever bar he's holed up in lately."

I nod. She's probably right about that. It's a wonder he hasn't come around to hit us up for money. I'm sure he knows Tim is doing well financially. I don't want to brag, but I'm sort of famous, too. Maybe he's ashamed. I decide not to worry about Dad anymore tonight, though. I keep thinking about whether Juniper was watching, what she thought about when she saw me score. I sigh.

"Hey, Gram, you wanna come with me tomorrow to Tim's office? I'm signing my contract and then we can get lunch. I'll buy!"

"Of course you'll buy, young man. You're living here rent free!" She whacks me with a pillow and I laugh.

"We'll head out around 11. Sound good?"

I check the locks and turn off the lights for Gram, falling into bed still thinking about how I'm more excited to see my lawyer in the morning than I was about scoring 2 goals in a Stanley Cup Playoff game. This chick feels more important to me than hockey right now, and that scares me shitless.

CHAPTER TWELVE
Juniper

"Here's to hockey!" Alice, the new chef at work, and I decided to go grab a beer after the Fury game. The entire staff of Stag Law was in the luxury suite to watch, and I have to admit it was pretty spectacular to see the game from that perch. I tried not to stare at Ty the entire time, but it's impossible to take your eye off the guy who has 10 shots at the goal.

My mind keeps wandering, thinking about how fierce Ty looked handling the puck. He played aggressively, and I could definitely see how he ran into trouble for fighting throughout his career. The other team kept trying to bait him, but a slap shot from the blue line straight into the goalie's five-hole was definitely a better answer than a punch to the jaw and a ride in the penalty box.

"Earth to Juniper! Hello!?"

"Oh man, I'm sorry Alice. I keep thinking about the game."

She smiles--she looks particularly happy tonight. "Me, too. And I don't even really like hockey!" Alice tells me about her family, how all of her siblings are so close. I love how warm and friendly she is and I'm glad she reached out to ask me for a drink after the game. She tells me that her sister and brother are in a fight over how high up they store the baseball bat, because her sister doesn't want her nephews to get hold of it. But as they were fighting, the boys got the bat and hit their uncle in the shins. I could listen to her stories about family for hours.

"Your house sounds like such a warm place," I say, and she nods. "I never had anything like that." I explain to Alice that it was just me and my dad growing up, but I don't have the energy to tell her the full story. I know that she lost her mom, though, so I tell her how my dad passed away a few years ago when I was in college. "It's just me now," I say, shrugging.

She smiles over her beer and pats my hand. "You and your new Stag Law family! But seriously, just come over sometime. I make way messier food when I'm at home, and I know you'll work it all off rowing anyway."

"Speaking of, I have to be on the water pretty early tomorrow. Sure you won't join us?"

Alice laughs. "I have enough going on. But I'll make you a good recovery shake for when you get to work. Deal?" I shake her hand and then we gather up our things and head home.

Lying in bed, I keep seeing scenes from the hockey game. I gripped the arms of my seat in the front row of the box, oblivious to everything around me, staring at Ty's face as he sped across the ice. The way he took control of the puck and the team around him reminded me of how he took charge that night in the bathroom. How he wouldn't stop until I was putty in his hands. Remembering, I can't help but slide my hand down my panties to feel the pulsing heat still thrumming there. I squirm, telling myself I shouldn't do this, but I can't escape my longing to feel him again. It doesn't take much--just a few flicks and I'm falling over the edge at the mere memory of Ty Stag and his magical body.

Monday morning I'm consulting with some other attorneys, divvying up some of the baseball contracts, when I hear a commotion in the hallway. I hear my boss scolding someone and then, there it is. The unmistakable voice of my notorious client, his brother. "Why is Ty here today?" I ask the room at large. They all shrug, but gather up their things as Tim opens the door in a huff.

"Juniper," he growls, "Can you come into my office?" *Shit. He doesn't know. This is about something else. Everything is fine.*

I walk in the hall and wait for the Stags to go ahead, but Ty pulls off to the side of the hall. "After you, Ms. Jones." He exaggerates his eye movements, dragging his gaze up and down my body, and I work very hard to maintain my composure.

"Mr. Stag," I say through gritted teeth, "Is there something I can help you with?"

His grandmother smacks him in the head, and I don't hold back the laugh that escapes my throat. "Tyrion, don't be a pig. Apologize right now."

Tim shoves his brother against the wall. "At least have the grace to look smug about getting called out. I told you to behave yourself here."

Ty shoves him back, saying, "You're just crabby because I flirted with your muffin chef."

"I told you to leave her the hell alone, too!"

I leave the Stag brothers to squabble in the hall and take a seat in Tim's office. Eventually they all come in, and Tim sits down.

"Juniper, ordinarily you wouldn't have to be here for Ty to

sign his playoff bonus contract, but I wanted to discuss a situation that has come up here with Stag Law."

Ty grabs the contract, scribbles a signature, and gets up as if to leave, but Tim asks him to stick around. "As you know we manage all aspects of our clients' legal needs, and--"

"Tim, spare us the boring part. Gram and I have lunch plans."

Tim frowns. "You'll hear later, I'm sure, that Jason Murdo was caught in a...situation."

Ty's eyebrows shoot up. "The baseball pitcher? What did he do?"

We all sigh, but Tim continues. "I'm going to be spearheading the situation with Murdo until we can resolve everything, and so that means I'm naming Juniper as our point person for all our NHL contracts."

I feel my jaw drop. "Wow, Tim, that's a huge gesture of trust from you."

"I don't anticipate this taking too long, but until it blows over, you'll be traveling with the teams for their away games. Donna can set you up with all the details for the travel account."

"Tim, I negotiated Friday flexibility as part of my salary with Stag Law. I have a regatta coming up and--"

"Juniper, you've got clients in the Stanley Cup finals and your company has another client facing prison. This is an extenuating circumstance, and you'll be awarded comp time, obviously."

Tim keeps talking and eventually shoos us out of his office so he can head down to the courthouse. I'm feeling stunned and disoriented again as I start walking with Ty and Mrs. Stag toward the elevators, not quite conscious of my actions, until Ty winks at me and says, "Don't worry, Junebug. I'll make sure we win each series in 4 games so this won't take very long."

I start to protest him calling me that, but the elevator door slides shut and he's gone.

CHAPTER THIRTEEN

Juniper

True to his word, Ty and the Fury are on fire. They sweep their playoff series and are up 3 games to 0 against the Dallas Knights. Some of the players wolf-whistled when I climbed onto their private plane the first time, but Ty stood up and screamed that I was their "fucking legal counsel" and called them a bunch of jagoffs. So that was interesting. Mostly I try to keep to myself on the road, meeting with team executives and hiding in my hotel gym, burning a hole in the treadmill.

I've missed several rowing practices now, and it seems unlikely that I'll be able to compete in the team's next regatta. I keep hoping Tim will finish things up with his baseball hotshot, but he's been wound up in court and bail hearings for weeks.

As a result, work is tense, too, when we're in Pittsburgh. I don't actually have much complicated legal work to do with my new group of NHL clients, but I'm finding there's a lot of communication with agents and legal departments from current or potential sponsors. Ben and Donna have both assured me that I'm catching on fast, and that my work is efficient, accurate, and meets the needs of my clients. So why do I feel so unsettled?

On the road in Denver, I don't get much sleep. After the Fury victory, I lie in bed in my hotel room trying not to think about how hot Ty looks all sweaty and happy, when my room phone and cell begin to ring simultaneously. I pick up the room phone, and a chorus of male voices floods into my ear. "Jooooooooniper! We neeeeeeeeed you!"

"What the hell?"

"Give me the phone. I said give me the fucking phone." I hear Coach's voice above what appears to be a herd of cattle in the background. "Juniper, I apologize."

"What's going on?"

"We need you. In an official capacity."

An hour later, I'm signing Hayden Murphy out of the drunk

tank at the Denver police station. The rest of the team is waiting outside on the sidewalk, leaning against sign posts, sloppy drunk to a man. I can't help but notice Ty isn't among them.

Hayden slumps over my shoulder, drunkenly saying, "You don't take any of the shit, do you?"

I shove him off me, and I'm strong enough that I succeed, which surprises him and causes the rest of the players to start cheering. "Listen," I shout at them.

They stop talking and stand straighter. "I'm going to bed. I don't want another one of these calls. Get drunk in your room if you must. Do not piss on other people's property. Is that clear?"

They collapse again in a fit of drunken laughter, and with Coach's help, I usher them into a set of minivan taxis he evidently called while I was in bailing out Murphy. I slump back to my hotel room, not sure whether to be relieved that Ty wasn't out with this gang of drunken fools.

Back in Pittsburgh, my office is filled with roses. My heart skips a beat, and then sinks when I see they're from Hayden. And Coach. Apologizing and thanking me for taking care of the disorderly charge and keeping it out of the press. Rather than enjoying the recognition for what was actually a lot of really delicate legal work, I feel foolish for hoping the flowers were from Ty. I guess this is my work now.

To make matters worse, I've been seeing Ty almost every day at the boat house when he's not on the road. Even with the playoffs, Ty's holding up his end of the image commitments. He hangs out at the boathouse, flirts with the team, and buys everyone new gear. And then, of course, I'm with the hockey team when they *are* on the road, which means I'm seeing a lot of Tyrion Stag these days.

The man is easy on the eyes, and that's a huge problem for me. I keep catching his stare on the plane, or else he'll catch me staring at him when we're in meetings or the team is viewing film before a game. I mostly try to ignore him at practice, which works about as well as when I try to ignore him all the time. I am totally unable to stop myself from behaving this way. I burn for this man. I need to talk to Tina or Alice, find out where I can meet some other men I can actually date. I wonder if Ben knows anyone...

This morning I have nowhere to hide. I came out to the river to row alone--it's an off day from team practices. My heart skips a beat when I see him leaning against the garage door, sipping his coffee and soaking up the early morning sun. I hate that I know he drinks his coffee with just a splash of milk. Two cups a day. I try to walk past him and just get to my workout, but he steps into my path.

"Knew you'd be here even on an off day, Junebug," he drawls, his grey eyes twinkling beneath his hat.

"We've discussed that name before, Stag." I brush past him as I unlock. He follows me inside.

"Yeah, and I decided I'm going to keep calling you that until I think of something better. Like Jonesy."

I snort.

"Nipper?" My face contorts in horror at the thought of that nickname, and Ty laughs. "Nah, not your style. Seriously, though, I had an idea about your training."

"Since when do you have any inside knowledge about rowing?" My voice is harsher than I intended, but I decide to blame the pressure from work.

He doesn't seem bothered by it and forges ahead, saying, "I don't know shit about rowing, but I'm a professional athlete. Surely you've noticed that I work out for a living. I've been talking to Derrick and learning some shit. And anyway, I noticed that nobody here ever records your trainings."

"Records them how?"

"Film, Juniper. Video? I spend hours every week watching myself skate. Someone records everything. Drills. Scrimmages. All of it. Then we sit with the coach and talk about it. Sooooo I thought I could record you rowing."

I pause in my task of lifting my boat from the rack. He's right, of course. Nobody films us. My father used to back in Boston. In high school, when I was making tapes for college teams, he would put together montages of me starting, mid-race, and finishing. But I haven't looked at my form on film in years. "All right," I say. "But you don't have anyone to take you out in the launch to record."

He grins, flashing a set of surprisingly straight teeth. "I thought of all that." He points to the deck of the boathouse. "I borrowed a camera from one of the film guys. If I stand on the deck there, I can record you for a long ways. If you circle the island, I can walk to the point there and catch you coming back around."

He really has given this a lot of thought, which both stuns and angers me for reasons I can't quite figure out. "What's your game here, Stag?" I cross my arms defensively. "Why would you do this for me?"

"No game, Juniper. Honest. I'm spending all this time here with you guys. Might as well help you up your performance, right?" He opens the duffel bag slung over his shoulder. "You going to let me record you?"

"Don't you have to go do a protein binge or carbo-load or something?"

He waves a hand at me. "I drank a shake on the way here," he says. "And before you ask, I have PT *after* practice and yesterday was strength day so no. I don't have to be in the weight room, either. I'm all yours this morning." Why is his grin so fucking irresistible? "We making movies or what?"

I sigh. "I guess I don't really have a choice about it." What I don't say is that I'm scared to see. That I'm so blown away by his offer I can barely think straight. This isn't some flirtatious gimmick. This is Ty offering something truly meaningful to me. *He wants to help me be a better rower.*

I really don't think anyone other than my dad has ever done something like this for me. I realize I've been standing still, just staring at him, so I shake my shoulders and get my boat in the water. I have no idea what my form looks like, haven't had individual coaching in years. He walks up the stairs to the deck and gives me a thumbs up once he's got himself situated. I shove off from the dock, planning to circle the island twice while he records and runs to his alternate viewing perch.

Like usual, I spend the first few minutes angry rowing. I'm pissed that I've missed team practices and might lose my seat to another rower who isn't as good as me, but shows up. I'm mulling over all my frustrations from work, trying to figure out why I'm irritated that Ty Stag seems to know his way around my mind *and* my crotch.

But as I find my rhythm, all those thoughts slip away. It's just me and the water again. I smell the river water, cool and brown in the morning haze. The muscles of my back and legs start to warm up from my efforts and when I enter the channel for my second lap, I decide I can really step up the pace. I glance over my shoulder and the way is clear as far as I can see. Grunting and pulling, I race toward downtown. I make my way around the southern tip of Herr's Island and ease up the oars, gliding back to the dock, gasping for breath.

I'm just pulling the scull from the water when Ty jogs down with his bag, grinning. I don't fully have my breath back yet, and I'm heaving a bit as I walk with the boat, but he follows me, saying, "That was awesome, Juniper. Seriously! Can we go sit inside and watch? My boy showed me how to hook the camera up to a laptop."

He reaches out a hand to steady my boat as I settle it on the rack. "I don't have my computer here with me," I say, frowning. "Can you email me the files?"

He shakes his head. "I don't know how to do that. Didn't you say you live just up the path or something? This won't take long and you can still be at work before my brother cracks the whip."

The thought of Ty Stag in my house sends my heart racing. I run through a mental scan of the townhouse. I haven't really been home enough to make a mess, but I know there's laundry all over my bedroom. He absolutely cannot see my bedroom. Or any space that would make him think about sex. I know it's impossible for me to be near him and not think about sex. He really shouldn't come to my house. But I want to see that film... Finally, I shrug and start walking toward home. Ty follows me, fiddling with the camera.

"This place has a great view," he says, grabbing my laptop from the kitchen counter before I can protest. He looks out the window to the porch, the panoramic view of the river outside, complete with the gentle sound of water lapping the banks. He settles himself onto my couch, spreading his long legs until there's barely any room for me if I don't want to touch him physically.

He spreads everything out on the coffee table, pops a cable into the laptop, and clicks the file that comes up on the screen. I wedge myself against the arm of the couch, trying not to think about how good he smells. Like sunshine and a little sweat. He must have really had to jog quickly between the deck and the lookout, because even though it's June, it's not hot out this early in the morning. Suddenly I feel shy realizing how hard he's working just to do something nice for me, and I'm treating him so suspiciously.

"There you are, Juniper," he says as I come onto the screen. At first it's awkward to watch, but soon I'm leaning forward, staring at myself. He points a thick finger at the screen and says, "Tell me what I should be looking at."

"Me looking," I tell him. Sure enough, I'm looking over my shoulder when the oars catch sometimes, or dipping one hand lower as my head swings back around. I explain to Ty that I should look over my shoulder while I'm driving my legs, to keep the boat stable. I'm describing what should be happening at the turn when I realize I'm totally leaning on Ty's leg with my elbows, as if it were a counter. The muscles are certainly as firm as the faux granite in my kitchen, but as soon as I'm aware of how close I am to his body, I jerk back.

"I really need to get ready for work," I say, my voice quiet.

Ty looks at where I'd been leaning against his leg and his hand slides to his lap. He nods and starts disconnecting the camera.

"Thank you, Ty, for the film. That's going to be really helpful for me."

"Any time, Juniper," he says. I can smell his breath, like mint gum and a very particular Ty-scent I shouldn't be remembering from the club bathroom. Then he says, "I like watching you." The air between us is charged. I can tell he wants to kiss me, and god! I want him. But it can't happen. I can't let it.

I stand up shakily. "Well, you probably need to get this camera back. Can you let yourself out? I'm going to shower before going to the office. Like you said, your brother's in a special mood these days..."

"Sure thing, Junebug," Ty says and winks. I rush into the bedroom and lean against the door with my eyes shut, as if that will help anything, and don't exhale until I hear my front door latch.

CHAPTER FOURTEEN

Ty

"Stag! Get in here!" Coach bellows to me as I limp past his office. Practice has been brutal this past week, but we're a few wins away from a Stanley Cup. This is exactly what I've trained for the last 20 years.

"Sure thing, Coach. What's up?"

"Don't give me that smug shit, Stag. Sit down." I can tell this isn't going to be a quick chat. I sigh, because I'd hoped to head to the boat house this afternoon and see if I could stare at Juniper's ass for awhile while she helped coach the high school kids.

Coach swivels his computer monitor toward me, pulling up a video. It's last night's game against St. Louis. Squinting, I see that he's been watching me and their winger, Houser. "I fuckin' hate that guy, Coach."

He frowns. "I know you do, Stag, and so does the rest of the NHL." Houser came up with me in the minors, was drafted the same year, and we've probably had more fights on the ice than anyone else I can think of. "I want to know what the hell you plan to do about it."

I shrug. Last night I managed to ignore him other than a few shoulder checks. "I'm not going to throw the first punch, Coach." I know what's on the line here. I've read my contract. Matty has been very clear. One fight and I'm gone. The Fury were the only team even willing to touch my contract, and that's just because they got a critical injury right before playoffs. Nobody wants a hothead they can't control. "I swear to God, I'll behave."

He scowls at me. "You're a loose cannon, Stag. Guys like you give the other teams power plays with the fighting and the penalties. And now Houser has something up his sleeve. I could smell it last night."

"I scored a hat trick twice so far in the playoffs," I snap back at him. "Look, I know my reputation is shit, but I've been festering in the minors for years now. I learned my lesson, I got the message, and I'm not going to fucking start with Houser. Remember how I wasn't there the night Murphy got arrested?" I shouldn't be smart mouthing to Coach like this, but he's not being fair.

He nods and scratches his chin. " Yeah, yeah. Good. Now get the hell out of my office and ice your hamstring."

I stagger down to the trainers, thinking how little I care about Houser, and how much Juniper is invading my thoughts lately. I've never met a girl who "got it" about sports. I don't have to explain anything to her, because she knows about timing my protein intake and stretching, the mental zone before a game. She does all that, too. It drives me wild. I could sit with her all day, watching her film, and not just because I like to look at her. When we were in her apartment, her face was so concentrated. I could see her analyzing every little thing in that video.

And then she leaned on my leg. Holy fuck, she leaned across my thigh and then told me she was getting into the shower. Naked. I had to go home and immediately take care of business as I remembered the feel of her pressed me.

I practically ran to my room and fell on the bed. I ripped down my shorts, panting, and started stroking myself, imagining it was her hand on my dick. I thought about the expression on her face when I made her come in the bathroom, could still smell her scent clinging to my clothes from sitting so close to her on the couch. In my fantasy, as I rubbed myself furiously, I imagined I actually did lean in to kiss her in her apartment. That she reached for my cock, kissed me back, stripped out of her sweaty clothes and straddled me. With one final tug, I felt the head of my cock swell and a thick stream of cum spurted into the air like the Point Park fountain, all over my clothes and my sheets. With a heaving sigh, I collapsed onto my bed as the last glimpse of my imagination faded--a memory of Juniper smiling, sexually sated.

God, soon, I think. *I have to have her again soon.* As I sink into the massage table, I reach for my phone to shoot her a text. **Can i ask u a favor @ the game 2morrow?**

> *This had better be related to my legal expertise*
> **Record me so we can watch and talk about my slap shot**
> *Doesn't the NHL pay people to do this for you?*
> **They don't smell as good as u**
> *Good night, Tyrion*
> **So you'll bring your camera tomorrow?**

She doesn't respond, and it takes all my restraint not to text her something crass about my text vibrating in her pocket.

My brother Tim is still wrapped up in the Murdo scandal, so

he's not at the game against St. Louis. It's a home game, for god's sake. He must be really tied up if he can't even come watch a home game. I know he'd rather be here with Thatcher and Gran, but part of me feels glad because I like Juniper sitting up in the box with my family. I know she's only here for work, but I like the look of her in a Stag jersey. I give her a wave when they announce my name, and I must have a shit-eating grin on my face because I can see Houser fucking staring at me across the ice. *Shit.* That's like rule number one. Never give those assholes something to bait you with.

There's no way he can know anything about Juniper, though. She could be anyone sitting up there next to my brother, with the agents and other families.

Every fucking faceoff, though, that asshole lays into me. "Who's your girlfriend, Stag?" "After we're done here, I'm going to show your girlfriend how a real man fucks." I sink a goal into the net right past his fucking skates and ignore him. The arena erupts. We're up 1-0 in the first period.

I can't help myself. I look up at the box again, smiling at my family, and then I lock eyes with Juniper. I see her blush and smile, and I remember why I became a professional athlete to start with. Moments like this. But I'm not just a superstar to her. She gets what it took to be here, how it fucking feels to score like that. She knows how I feel right now. I'm grinning like a lunatic, which is why I don't even see it coming when Houser clocks me from behind.

I don't know how I keep my feet, but I sway, giving him time to toss off his gloves and come at me again. This time, I'm ready and my conscious mind goes dormant. I'm totally in primal mode. I don't even know how many times I hit him. Both our helmets have flown off at this point and I can see blood flying. I land an uppercut under Houser's jaw and he flies backward. The ref comes in to break it up, dragging me over to the penalty box.

When I look over at Coach, he draws a hand across his neck and I know I fucked it all up. After my two minutes is up, the team manager comes to escort me down the tunnel. *Shit, they're not even letting me finish the fucking game,* I think. "Coach, he hit me first. He fucking started it, Coach."

Coach turns away from me, which pisses me off. Murphy and Kingston stare down at their skates. This isn't fair and they all know it. I've done my part. I reined it in. All I've done wrong is lust after my lawyer, and I'm pretty sure none of them know that. I think. Now I'm not being allowed to play hockey, and I'm wild with rage. I see red and start kicking the wall with my skate on. Fuck that guy. Shit. My whole body hurts from that fight.

I see Matty come charging down the tunnel and he pulls me

aside. "Ty, baby, Houser says he's pressing charges for assault."

I actually laugh, because the thought is so ridiculous. But Matty tells me the entire thing is under review, and I can't be on the ice until they reach a decision. "Where's your attorney, Ty?"

"You know where she is, Matty. Why do I need a fucking attorney for this? It's a god damned hockey fight that I didn't even start."

"You didn't drop your stick when Houser hit you the first time," he explains. I can't even remember. It came out of nowhere. When did I drop the stick? Is he seriously trying to claim I used my stick as an assault weapon? Matty's long face tells me this is really happening. My jaw drops and for the first time, I'm worried they're going to end my career over some stupid technicality after I got sucker punched.

CHAPTER FIFTEEN

Juniper

"What the hell is happening?" I lean over to Thatcher Stag as I see some officials hauling Ty out of the arena. He shrugs. "Surely this isn't typical after a fight?"

I hear the door slam and through the windows of the box, I see Matty running down the hall. I sigh and reach for my bag. I do a quick mental scan through Ty's contract, remembering he has a morality clause in there and specific language about instigating a fight. They're replaying the whole thing on the jumbo screen again, so I can see quite plainly that Ty was sucker punched by the St. Louis player.

My phone starts to vibrate and I see that it's Ty's agent. "Matty, what's going on?" He shouts some nonsense about a dropped stick and tells me to get down to the locker room.

By the time I reach Ty, the press is swirling around trying to get a comment. I can barely push my way through and Matty yanks me into the room and slams the door on the reporters.

"This is clearly an intimidation tactic by a bunch of sore losers," Matty declares. I'm sure he's right. St. Louis is about to lose their third game in a row and the Fury are basically clinching the Cup...but I'm only concerned about my client right now.

"So what do we do about it?"

It turns out we just sit around and wait until the officials can all agree that Houser's claims are utterly bogus. Meanwhile, the game has continued and St. Louis has enjoyed 25 minutes of ice time without the Fury's leading goal scorer. It's a pretty brilliant strategy on their part, I guess. Bait and attack the notorious hothead. Get him out of the way. If you can't win with talent, I guess you have to resort to this kind of thing.

"This is bullshit," I say. "Where is Ty?"

Matty waves over in the direction of the training room. I'm

desperate to see him, and I can't tell where my professional obligation to him ends and my personal care for him begins, but when I walk in the room and see him wincing in pain as the trainer treats a cut, I just about lose it.

His face is swollen and bruised, his lip cut. His knuckles look like raw meat. He must have gotten Houser in the teeth with his fist. I reach out a tentative hand to touch his cheek, thinking to comfort him I guess, but he stiffens beneath my touch. The trainer looks at me with a raised eyebrow.

I clear my throat. "I'm the lawyer. And this is ridiculous. We should charge *him* with assault. Don't think I won't do it."

Ty puts his good hand on my arm. "Juniper. It's a hockey fight. We aren't pressing charges. I just want to fucking play in the game. I don't even want to take revenge." The trainer looks concerned again. "I swear! I just want to fucking play."

I pat his arm and look him right in the grey, swollen eyes. "I'm going to make sure that happens, Ty. I promise." I set my jaw and run through my options. I straighten up to my full height and Ty smiles.

"Matty!" I yell and march back across the locker room. "Show me where these assholes are making decisions."

Matty grabs security to walk me back into the arena. The game has restarted. "This is unacceptable," I mutter. Now the lawyer in me is fired up. This is injustice. I'm pissed.

Even though I have no idea what's going on, I shove my way past all the security guards back in the arena, over to the off-ice officials. "Excuse me, I'm the legal representation for Tyrion Stag. I demand to know what's going on and why the game is being allowed to continue while his status is in limbo."

Six heads whip in my direction and I can see a group of suits approaching. I don't care that I'm wearing a hockey jersey with jeans. My client is being treated unfairly, and this is why I'm here. I demand that the video judge run back the footage of the incident, and within a few minutes, I've threatened to sue the management of the St. Louis team. Not for assault. For fixing the game. That shuts them up real fast.

Ty is reinstated, and I'm still on an adrenaline rush when I return to the locker room to tell him so. Everyone around me cheers and starts patting me on the back, but Tyrion Stag picks me up and kisses me.

My heart stops. My body longs to respond. I want to melt into his soft lips, plunge my tongue into his mouth. He's so passionate, and I fully admit it was a huge turn on when he smiled at me after scoring his goal. But I'm here at work, and my senses all fire warning signals. I squirm out of his arms and slap him.

He seems stunned and looks around the room, where everyone is staring, slack-jawed. "I'm sorry, Juniper. I got carried away." His voice shakes.

I can't find words, but Matty laughs nervously and says, "We're all a little over excited here, Ty. No worries, baby. Get your ass back out there."

I spend the rest of the night praying that Tim will be done with his baseball scandal in time for the next game. The Fury win 4-1 with Ty scoring another goal in the third period. I'm terrified to think what will happen if I have to travel with the team and find myself in the same hotel as him after another victory. My lips still tingle from his kiss long after the arena is empty.

Matty calls the next day to report that Ty is getting benched for the next game. "Matty, that's ridiculous. He was sucker punched!" I protest, but Matty explains that they can't afford to have something like that happen again or play short-handed.

"They'd rather play a full roster than risk Ty in the sin-bin for extended time periods and lose because of power plays," Matty says. This is a team decision, and I can't do a thing about it, legally, and I hate that.

After work, I take out all my frustrations on the water. I've missed so many team practices now that I told Derrick I was withdrawing myself from the women's boat. I'm just rowing solo when I can fit it in. I'm surprised to see Ty standing on the dock when I get back from my row.

"Hey," he says, sitting down.

"Hey yourself," I reply. "I'm so sorry, Ty. I did everything I could to fight this."

He nods. "I know you did, Junebug. The whole NHL is talking about what a stone-cold demon you were with those officials." He grins at me and I feel slightly better. But his smile isn't a fully happy smile. He sighs and asks, "Want to watch the game with me on TV somewhere?"

I nod. "Can you wait while I change?"

"Can you just throw on a jersey and watch some hockey all sweaty?" I roll my eyes at him, but when he hands me a Stag jersey I toss it on and follow him up the bike path to one of the bars that is broadcasting the playoff game on the big screen on the deck. Ty pulls his hat low over his eyes and keeps his sunglasses on, trying to avoid being recognized.

Should I ask him about the kiss? I can't read his face. I've never seen him like this before. My heart aches for him. I see him nervously drumming his fingers on the table.

"Ty." He looks over at me. His expression breaks my heart and I can't help myself. I reach out and squeeze his hand. He doesn't let go, just holds it while the game plays on without him.

We sit in silence and watch as the Fury lose 1-0.

CHAPTER SIXTEEN

Juniper

A week and a Fury comeback later, of course, Tim is still neck deep in his cocaine case and I have to fly to St. Louis for the final game.

I have Lisa on video chat, filling her in on everything that's happened with Ty as I figure out what to pack. "So you held hands? For like an hour? Then what happened?"

"Then he walked me home and patted me on the back like I was a teammate. He turned away and jumped in his car and took off. Hey, do you think I need anything dressy?"

She nods and reminds me there might be some sort of victory party I need to attend. Shit.

"Juniper, I don't even know this guy, but I already like him so much better than Zack. Like, before I even knew that Zack was screwing around on you, that guy gave me the creeps."

This is news to me. "Wouldn't have killed you to say something to me about it," I say.

"Girl, you know you can't tell your friends you don't like their partner. Then I'd turn into the bitch who didn't like your spouse and you'd stop talking to me. But it doesn't matter because I like *this* guy. He filmed you rowing, Juney. He *helped* you."

"Well it doesn't matter because I can't be with him unless I figure out a way to get Tim to reassign him to another lawyer. Which I can't do if I don't ever get to talk to him--he's neck deep in this court case w the damn baseball player." I sigh. "I wish your brother and I could just swap clients."

"Tell my brother I approve of this plan," Lisa says. "Whatever gets my Juniper laid."

I hang up with Lisa and drive to the airport, where I get to go through a special security line and off to the terminal for the Fury's private flight. This will never get old. I'll admit, I am still pretty starstruck by the whole process. This whole being treated like royalty bit? I could get used to this. The players are all taking selfies with the flight crew, signing autographs. I check in with Coach and the executive team, briefly review the legal needs for the trip: none unless the guys get drunk and piss on someone's porch again. I slide my tablet into my bag and get ready to board the plane. I don't even make eye contact with Ty.

He's got his hat pulled low, his headphones on. I can tell he's deep in concentration, getting ready for game mode. I don't want to interfere with this. He's coming back from an emotional hit, his hand still looks a mess, and this game could clinch the cup if they win. No pressure, right? Ha. The air is full of it. It smells of anxiety and confidence and testosterone. I can actually smell it.

I sit way up front and spend the whole flight reading a romance novel. At least someone is getting a happily ever after.

On game night I head up to the executive suite with Matty and the Stag family. Well, all of them but Tim. Thatcher seems to have brought a date, who is not wearing enough clothing to keep warm in an ice cold arena, but that doesn't seem to be the point.

Anna Stag smiles and waves me over. "Mrs. Stag," I say, shaking her hand. "How was your flight? Are you in the team hotel?"

"Fine, fine. Timmy put me up in a fancy room. They put a mint on my pillow. Did you ever have that?"

I shake my head. "I got a bag of popcorn on the night stand, though." This friendly rapport with Ty's grandmother seems oddly inappropriate, but she's nice so I try to roll with it. She gives a harsh look to Thatcher, who shrugs and puts his arm around his date. Mrs. Stag says, "I wish they'd just get started already. I really want to watch Tyrion win this thing!"

"Me, too. Trust me!" I've had about enough of meeting with stuffy NHL officials who all think I'm a heinous bitch. Every time one of them catches my eye, I see them twitch. At all our pre-game meetings, when I bring up unsavory and questionable player discipline procedures, they wince. Good. They've all behaved like assholes. Let them think what they want about me. My client is playing tonight.

I waffle about texting Ty before the game. I don't want to distract him when he's doing his mental prep, but I feel a deep yearning to connect with him. He hasn't spoken to me since he walked me home after we watched the game together. I sigh and pull out my phone, typing **Just wanted to let you know I gave STL legal counsel the full Juniper treatment. There shouldn't be any funny business tonight.**

Glad u got my back. He adds an emoji of a dragon. I smile.

This is what you pay me for. Good luck out there, Ty.

Thanks for being here, JJ.

God, I'm blushing like a teenager, I think. Eventually, the anthems and the speeches end and the puck drops. I only have eyes for Ty. He's everywhere on the ice, and I'm sure he's moving so fast his blades are melting the surface. It's hard not to get caught up in the excitement of being here. Is it the high profile game or is it just Ty?

I spend the next three hours pressed against the glass of the suite, rapt. My body yearns for Ty as I watch him on the ice. He moves so gracefully, with such precision and purpose. He is aggressive and confident, and I hear him shouting out calls to his teammates, intercepting passes I didn't even see coming.

I can see exactly why the Fury sought him out despite his reputation for fighting. He brings the Fury together, acts like the spark they all need to function as a unit. He's passionate and animated, shouting to his teammates as he glides by, calling out plays. He doesn't score in this game, but gets 2 assists, and when the final buzzer sounds, the Fury win 3-2. The best in the league. They won the cup. I actually tear up, I'm so excited for him. I know he's worked for this since he was 3 years old and started bruising through junior hockey leagues.

And I know I don't just feel happy for him as his lawyer. I want *him.* I want this man who cares enough about me to help me with my athletic performance. I want the funny guy who tries to think up annoying nicknames for me. I want the man who smells like mint and pine and citrus. I want him and he's off limits.

This is his moment, but when they start the awards ceremony for the Stanley Cup, I know I can't bear to watch as he starts partying with his teammates. I don't want to think about him slurping champagne from the cup with some bimbo.

Amidst the chaos of celebration in the suite, I slip away back to the hotel to be alone with my thoughts. My feelings for Ty aren't appropriate. He's my client at the job I need...I cannot leave two jobs in one year, and especially not because of men. I don't even know what's going on with Ty. Infatuation? Is it just lust because I've never had a sexual experience like I had with him?

I feel terribly alone as I sink into my bed, wishing I had someone I could confide in about this. I can't call Lisa at this hour--she has a regatta in the morning. She'll have gone to bed hours ago. My feelings about Ty are so much more than just a lustful romp in a bar bathroom. We've gotten so close at rowing practices and elsewhere, and I can talk to him about "clean eating" and interval training. I'm desperate to be around him, to make him smile, to hear his thoughts. My tears are on the verge of falling, the knot in my throat about to give way to sobs, when I hear a knock at the door of my hotel room.

CHAPTER SEVENTEEN

Ty

I didn't even have to work hard to get the girl at the desk to give me Juniper's room number. It's not like I flirted with her. I just asked nice. Sometimes you have to swing your celebrity status around. Eye on the prize. Juniper is the ultimate prize. I need her, right now, or I'm going to lose my mind.

I loosen my tie as I wait for Juniper to come to the door. I hear her shuffle up and see her eye look through the peephole, hear her little intake of breath when she sees that it's me.

"Juniper, open up," I whisper, not even sure why I'm bothering to keep my voice down.

She opens the door and she looks a mess, and I love it. She's still wearing a jersey with my name on the back, but she took off her jeans, so all I'm seeing are those long legs sticking out from the black and gold fabric. "Fuck, Juniper, you look so good right now."

"Ty, what are you doing here?" her face looks concerned, upset.

I shrug. "Do you want me to leave?"

She hesitates, then shakes her head no. "Shouldn't you be out celebrating with your team?"

I push my way into the room and close the door behind me, not taking my eyes off her. "Juniper Jones, you're the only one I want to be with tonight." I close the gap between us so I'm standing an inch away from her, breathing in the scent of her arousal, looking into her eyes as her pupils dilate. She bites her lip. I lean in to whisper right against her ear. "And I want to celebrate by licking every inch of your body and fucking you while you're wearing my jersey."

She gasps, and I press my mouth against hers. I pull back and ask, "Do you want that, Jonesy? Do you want me to fuck you tonight?"

Her mouth works up and down like she's thinking about it,

and I hesitate, but she finally whispers, "Yes." All bets are off now. I don't care about hockey or my brother or anything except tasting this woman. Her mouth opens and I slip my tongue inside, running it slowly against her teeth while my hands explore that beautiful body.

Her tits are so firm in my hands and I feel her nipples pebble through the jersey material. *No bra,* I realize, and I feel my dick swell in my pants. I hook a hand under her knee and back her up until we tumble onto her bed. God, it feels good to lie on top of her.

She's kissing me back in earnest now, and it's so hot when I feel her get excited by what we're doing. Her hands are fumbling with my shirt and tie, so I pull up onto my knees to shed as many layers as I can while Juniper sits halfway up to watch. "You like what you see," I tease, moving more slowly as I unbutton the dress shirt I had to stick on for press interviews after the match.

She grabs me by the tie and pulls me back down to kiss her as her hands dip to open my pants. I moan when she finds what she's looking for and wraps her fist around my cock. "That feels so good, babe." I kick my pants the rest of the way off and climb back between her legs, fully naked now against her silky skin.

I want to touch and taste all of her, and I waste no time getting started. She moves to take the jersey off and I shake my head. I take her wrist in my hand and bring it to my mouth, planting soft kisses on the sensitive skin at the base of her palm until she gasps. "Keep the jersey on." I make my way down her body, sliding my tongue along each curve, each firm muscle. Juniper lifts her hips as I slide off her little black panties and then I hear her suck in her breath as I toss her legs over my shoulders.

I settle on my knees at the foot of the bed and slowly, gently spread legs her open. "So beautiful," I say, my voice a rumble. Juniper is quivering and I grin at her. "You want me to touch you there, don't you?"

She nods. I run the pads of my fingers gently along her upper thighs, teasing, growing closer and closer to her center, but never quite touching her. I want to make this last. I want to see her let go, to make her fall apart, and then I'll be there to pick up the pieces. Finally, she throws her head back and bucks her hips up toward my hand. "Jesus, Ty, will you fucking touch me?" Her voice is guttural and I can see she's going nuts with want.

"I am touching you, baby," I tease, grazing my nails along her stomach, the tops of her thighs again. "Did you want me to touch you somewhere specific?"

She pulls my hair. I'm still in no hurry. And fuck, I want to hear her mouth say exactly what she wants from me.

"Ty! Please. Touch my clit. Please."

"There now, Junebug. Was that so hard?" I circle her clit

gently with one finger, adjusting my weight, getting ready to taste her.

When I bend to kiss her pussy, she screams as my tongue finds home on her neat little bud. I work her clit with my tongue gently, savoring the taste and feel of her. I've finally got her body beneath me and trembling. For me. I fucking love this. I turn my head to gently lick her inner thighs where the skin is soft and so, so sensitive. She tremors, muttering and saying my name again and again, begging me to return to her clit, but I want to draw this out. I've waited so long to be here. As I make my way up her legs with my tongue, so slowly, I gradually put my hands under her ass, slowly kneading her cheeks. I love how each cheek fills my hands, and I have big fucking hands. I start licking her everywhere except her clit, but every so often I thrust my tongue inside her as deep as I can. Juniper moans and gasps and I feel her legs reacting as the super sensitive skin makes contact with the stubble on my cheeks. She's wide open for me, so wet, and I slide a finger inside, crooking it toward me while I lap at her with my tongue.

I can feel my dick weeping pre-cum as the sight of Juniper losing her mind turns me on. I love that I'm able to do this to her, make her let go, bring her this pleasure. I can tell Juniper is close. "Please, Ty. Please. Fucking touch me. Make me come, Ty!"

I growl at the sound of her begging this way, and start to gently suck on her clit, holding it so gently between my teeth. I know this is working for her because she slams her knees against my head, holding me in place with those iron thighs of hers. I feel her hands in my hair and hear her screaming, "Fuck, fuck, fuck! Ty! Yes!!!" I lick her harder, pumping my hand faster, and when I can tell she's almost there, I suck on her clit just that much harder. I pull back just a little to blow cool air on her clit while I speed up the finger that's pumping in and out of her center. I feel her whole body tense and she grasps the sheets, thrashing around like wild.

"Ty!" She yells. "Ty, I'm going to come. Oh God!!!" And I feel her contracting around my hand. I rock back on my heels, just watching her, enjoying her ecstasy. I slide my hands to her thighs and I feel her pulse racing, see her chest heaving as she tries to regain her composure. Finally, she opens her eyes and smiles at me, and I realize I'm not just lusting after this   woman.   I'm   falling   for   her.

CHAPTER EIGHTEEN
Juniper

He broke me. I'm sure of it. I just crumpled into a thousand pieces and I will never be able to move again. I'm not even sure what just happened there, because nobody has ever done anything like that to me before. Ever.

I feel Ty gently placing my legs back on the bed, kissing his way back up my body until he's lying between my legs again, chest hovering above mine with his weight on his forearms. I love the feel of him on top of me, big and heavy and firm. He's got about five inches of height on me, but lying this way, our foreheads line up and I stare into his eyes. As his hand gently strokes my side, I feel goosebumps raise on my skin. I also feel like I want more. "I want you inside me," I say.

He nods and reaches for his pants on the floor next to the bed. He pulls out a strip of condoms and I laugh. "Did you stop at the drugstore on the way over here?"

He grins until his dimples appear. He slowly and carefully opens the wrapper and rolls the condom onto his massive cock. "They were in all our lockers after the game," he says. He nestles back on top of me, his sheathed tip at the entrance to my heat. "I'm going to use all of them tonight, Juniper."

"Mmm, yes, please."

He kisses me as he slides inside and I groan into his mouth. He tastes like champagne and...oh shit. He tastes like me. I can taste myself on his mouth and it turns me on. He begins to move inside me and I lift my hips to meet each of his thrusts. Oh God, this feels exquisite. Fucking him in the bathroom was hot and fierce. But this is something else entirely. As we move together, it's hot and needy and so personal. His big cock fills every inch of me, but even more than that I feel him connecting with me mentally. This big hockey guy who knows what makes me tick as a rower, who always has a smile for me and makes me come until my eyes roll back

57

into my head. I feel how much he wants this. With me. I feel how he has longed for this, maybe as much as I have. "That's it, Juniper. Wrap those long fucking legs around me, baby." I comply, eagerly, pinning him against me so tightly, grinding against his pelvic bone to find the friction I need.

Suddenly, he freezes. "What's wrong?" I gasp.

But he shakes his head, looking around the room. "I want to watch," he says. He pulls out and stands up and, before I know what's happening, he lifts me and carries me to the dresser by the mirror. He places me at the very edge and stands between my legs, sliding into me again. *Oh, yes.* I lock my legs around his back and cling to his shoulders, the wooden edge of the dresser digging into my thighs as he fucks me. My nails press into the muscles of his back, trail along to his chest as he groans. Looking up into his face, I follow his gaze to the wall mirror, where the sight of us fucking is enough to send me over the edge again.

We look amazing together. His rippling muscles gleam with a sheen of sweat and the jersey with his name on it is bunched up so he has access to my breasts, to all of me. I'm clinging to him to stay upright and I can see my muscles shake with the force of him thrusting into me.

"Ty!" I shout his name, groaning and moving against him. I wrap my arms around his neck for support and his hands brace his weight on either side of me. The dresser slams into the wall--we are being so loud-- but I can't even care about that as wave after wave of electricity shocks through my body. I'm so wet. I can feel my desire coating his cock. He slips in and out of me and it feels so damn good.

Ty speeds up his pace, pummeling into me, and I love to watch his muscles flex and move. I should have been fucking athletes years ago. This is amazing. And just like that, he grabs my chin and turns my head so I'm staring into his eyes. I fear he can see right inside me. His grey eyes are fierce and I feel him redouble his efforts. I can't believe he's able to go faster, harder. I squeeze my own muscles, trying to draw him into me and hold him as tightly as I can. "Fuck, Juniper, that's hot," he growls. "You're so fucking wet." He pulls out again and quickly twists my body around so I'm bending over the dresser.

Ty stands behind me and lifts the hem of his jersey, his big hands massaging the globes of my ass. When he slams back into me, the impact makes my tits jiggle. He holds me tight with one forearm, pressing his chest against my back while he pounds into me, and I love it. I love every thrust. From this angle, his cock rubs against some secret spot inside me that makes me erupt. My eyes roll up in my head as I scream and when his other hand moves from my ass to rub my clit, I lose whatever control and consciousness I had left. I feel my hips bucking back against his until he shudders and shouts "Yes! Juniper I'm fucking cumming. I'm cumming so hard, baby."

I can feel his cock swelling inside me. I feel him emptying himself into the condom. I gasp for breath, exhausted, and collapse against the dresser.

He kisses my neck while we both catch our breath, then steps away from me. Immediately, I miss the heat of his body. I feel like my knees are going to give, and a few seconds later, I see Ty toss the condom in the garbage. Then he tugs me down onto the bed beside him and touches me so gently, stroking my arm, my hair, my cheek. I've never felt so satisfied, so safe. We just fucked like beasts, and yet it felt so personal and so much more real than anything else I've ever done with a man.

"What are you thinking about," he asks as he gently tickles the skin of my back, up inside the jersey. I shake my head, but he insists. "If you don't tell me, I won't fuck you again, Juniper."

I can't help but laugh, and when he rolls me to face him, I bite my lower lip and take a deep breath. "I was just thinking I didn't know it could be like that."

His hand stills. "Like what?"

I shrug. "Like whatever the hell that was."

Now his eyes light up and he puts his thumb against my lower lip. Instinctively, I draw it into my mouth, sucking on his massive digit. He smiles, and I could stare into his eyes all day like this. He asks, "Are you saying I gave you the best sex of your life," twisting his other hand into my hair. I nod and keep sucking his thumb, and even though we just finished having sex a moment ago, I feel him stiffen against my hip.

"Well, shit, Juniper. If I knew the bar was so low, I wouldn't have worked so hard." I love the feel of his laugh echoing through his chest. He begins stroking my hair and I close my eyes, feeling safe and secure in an unfamiliar way I don't want to end.

We lie still for a few minutes. I start to fall asleep, but hear him say something. "Tell me your story, Juniper Jones," he whispers.

"What do you mean?"

"Like how did you get into rowing? Start there."

I explain that my dad was an Olympic rower, that rowing wasn't optional at my house, but he wants to know about the first time, the way I knew I loved it, all of that. I sigh. "I've never talked about this part before," I tell him, and he looks into my eyes, expectantly.

"Well you said you never came like that before, either, right?" His steel grey eyes focus on mine and I'm mesmerized by him, drawn in as always. I feel myself spilling my deepest secrets, telling Ty that I don't actually know who my birth parents are, that all my conscious memories begin in foster care and group homes around Boston. "I have no history," I tell him, choking back a tear.

"But you have a dad, you said..."

I nod. "When I was 12, my school took a field trip to the boat house. Who even knows if it was just a stop along the day or what. Anyway, my dad was there volunteering. He saw the other students picking on me." I tell Ty how I was fascinated by the oars, by the rowers we saw on the water. I raised my hand to ask question after question, making myself stand out. "Anyone who stood out for whatever reason...that's who got hurt. It didn't matter if you had a toy the others wanted, or if you were more beautiful than the other girls so the house father gave you special attention..." I have to pause here and gather my wits. Special attention from the foster fathers was the worst part of it. I'd do anything to avoid that. Anything. "Or the house mother beat you for her own lost ambitions. If you cared too much about whatever you were learning in school. Anything, Ty. Anything that made you stand out got you hurt."

I feel him grit his teeth when I describe growing up like that, but he presses me to tell him more about the day I discovered rowing, about that field trip to the boat house.

The kids bided their time and didn't realize anyone was watching. "They shoved me into the river, and my dad grabbed an oar and knocked their legs out from under them, then used the oar to haul me in," I tell Ty, smiling. We both laugh at this mental image.

"He must have been one tough son of a bitch," Ty says. I nod.

"Dad was in his 60s when he adopted me. He took me into the boat house to dry off, found out I was an orphan, and started the process to adopt me that day. Said he saw a fire in me that he admired."

"What happened to him?"

I roll away from Ty, facing the wall to hide my tears. It's still raw to talk about. "He died a few years ago," I manage to choke out. "I only got   him   for   ten   years."

CHAPTER NINETEEN

Ty

"God, Juniper, I'm sorry," I tell her, kissing her neck and rubbing her shoulders. "You know, I know how it is to lose a parent. That shit will fuck with your head for years. What you described? Being in all those houses? That could have been me and my brothers if Tim hadn't stepped up and gotten my grandmother to move in with us." She doesn't say anything then and I just hold her close, telling her stories about my family. How Tim basically raised us while my dad drank away his grief and our income.

"And all I did was give Tim shit, too," I say. "He will tell you he fought to get me into schools that had good hockey programs, but the truth is I would have gotten kicked out of all the other schools. Hockey was the only way I could beat the shit out of people and not wind up in juvie." I sigh. "Hey, Juniper?"

"Mmm?"

"I'm glad you wound up in Pittsburgh and found me in the bar that night." I hadn't meant to exploit this moment, seeing as both of us just spilled the beans about our dead parents, but I'm totally overcome by my feelings for this woman right now. There's never been anyone who could relate to me about this stuff before, on top of understanding all the other things that make me tick.

But I can't help what my cock is doing, and right now it's growing hard nestled between Juniper's ass cheeks. I'm prepared to walk away and hop into a cold shower, but she wiggles her hips around, nudging against me in a way that shows me she's down for some distraction sex.

I roll onto my back, and Juniper sits up. She takes off the jersey then and holy shit, her tits are amazing. I pull her against my chest and roll on top of her, rubbing the silken expanse of her front, letting my rough hands tease along her skin. I love how solid she is beneath me. She's firm and perfect. I don't have to worry that I'm going to break her. I can just lose myself in the moment. She starts to moan in pleasure and when she

61

reaches down to palm my length, I groan right along with her.

I reach for the strip of condoms on the nightstand and tear open the next one in the line. "We've still got a lot of work to do, baby," I whisper, wrapping myself in latex. Then she shoves me back on the bed and straddles me. I look up to see all of Juniper rising above me, like a goddess, before she slides down onto me with her warm, waiting folds.

In this position, locked together face to face with her on top, I just have to rock my hips slowly and it feels so tight, so deep, so good. Juniper sways her hips along with my mine and I smile. "We're moving together like rowers," I say, laughing.

She plants a kiss on my mouth, then bites my lip. "No crew jokes until you make me come again, Stag."

"Yes, ma'am," I tell her, and waste no time getting us both across the finish line.

After, I'm feeling pretty spent, what with having played a Stanley Cup Final and fucking my attorney ten ways to Tuesday. I lie on my back with my hands laced together under my head, hoping to catch some shuteye, but I feel Juniper staring at me. "What?" I ask, cracking open one eye.

Her short hair is tousled and messy. Her lips are swollen from my kisses and her eyes are glassy, like she's stoned on post-orgasmic fumes. She says, "Are you actually going to stay?"

This takes me by surprise. "Babe, I have no intention of moving."

"You're going to spend the night? I didn't think Tyrion Stag did things like that." She looks skeptical.

"Tonight was a first for me in a few ways." I laugh. It feels good to laugh with a woman. I guess we're getting ready to have a conversation again, because she starts tracing the tattoo on my chest.

"A stag?" She touches the leaping stag above my heart. My brothers and I all have the same tattoo. Thatcher designed it and the day I turned 18, we all went together to get it.

"He's leaping over laurel," I tell her. "That was my mom's name. Laurel." I bring her hand to my lips and kiss her fingers. She strokes my cheek with her other hand, and instead of recoiling from this intimacy, I want to soak it in. With her.

I reach over her again and turn off the light so we're immersed in darkness. I pull her close against me and adjust the blankets to fight off the chill from the hotel air conditioning. "We still have one more condom to use later," I whisper into her ear. "Now get some rest."

I feel her smile even though I can't see her face, and as we are drifting off it occurs to me that Juniper doesn't have to be up early tomorrow...because she's here for my athletic event and missing hers as a consequence. "Hey," I ask her. "What's up with your crew team? Don't you have a big regatta this week?"

I feel her stiffen. "Well, I've had to miss a lot of practice," she says. "I ceded my seat to Jamie after Tim told me about the Murdo situation. I've been rowing alone to stay in shape but I'm not going to be able to compete tomorrow."

"Aw Juniper, you can't miss your race for me."

She scoffs. "I'm not. I'm missing my race for my boss." In a rush, the reality of us comes crashing down on me. She can get fired for being here with me. What was the phrase she used? Ethics violation? Juniper can get disbarred, I guess, which means she can't be a lawyer anymore. Hell, more than missing a race for me, she could lose her entire career for taking a risk with me tonight.

"There has to be a way," I say. "Let me talk to my brother."

"Ty, you must not, under any circumstances, tell your brother that we slept together. Do I make myself clear?"

I nod, seeing the glint in her eyes even in the sliver of light that creeps into her hotel room from under the door. She's my secret then, I guess. She feels like one worth keeping.

She rolls over, putting a little distance between us in the bed, but she doesn't kick me out of her room. I think about how much her career means to her, how she doesn't have any family left and really, all she cares about is her job and her rowing. Now both of those things are at risk because of me. I want to do something nice for her, to let her know she can count on me. Not just for sex. I let my fingers trace lines down her spine, feeling the strong muscles of her back, and I get an idea.

CHAPTER TWENTY

Ty

As soon as the light of dawn slips through the crack in Juniper's curtains, I start waking her up the best way I know how: morning sex. God, I love how tall she is. She fits right up against me, so solid. I slide into her from behind, lying on our sides, where I can kiss her neck and suck on her ear lobe until she practically purrs. Once we've used the last of the condoms, I tell her to get cleaned up and put on her workout clothes.

"I don't really feel like going to the gym right now, Ty," she says, but I roll her out of bed. I need to make a call, and I need her out of the room if I'm going to surprise her.

While Juniper gets herself ready in the bathroom, I call up the number listed on the website for the St. Louis rowing club. I swing my celebrity status around again and offer them a very generous donation if they can find a single boat for Juniper to borrow for an hour this morning to get in her workout.

Once she's ready to go, I tell her to go ahead and check out and meet me back at my room. "You can stash your stuff there until your flight," I tell her, and when she looks concerned, I've got that figured out, too. "I've got to meet a sponsor for lunch, and I'd really like my attorney to accompany me and make sure they're not trying to fuck me. Contractually."

She laughs, but I can tell she's still nervous about getting caught with me. "Just give me your bag, go check out, and I'll meet you in the lobby in ten minutes," I say, and this seems to sit better with her.

I put on my suit pants and undershirt, not caring a bit that anyone who sees me in the hall knows exactly how I spent my night. Most of the hotel guests are with the Fury anyway. Up in my room, I brush my teeth and change, tossing J's bag in the corner, and grabbing my wallet.

I pull on some dark shades and a ball cap, hoping to be at least a little incognito while the lobby is still buzzing after last night's game. Word seems to have leaked out that the Fury are staying here, and the place is crawling with photographers--both professional and iPhone paparazzi. I see Juniper sort of hiding behind a plant and I sidle up behind her, whispering "you should pick a taller fern if you're looking for camouflage."

She shakes out of my grip, looking angry or terrified or both. "Come on," I tell her. I move to take her hand but she looks like she's going to hit me again. I throw my hands up, "woah, babe. I called a car service. We can go out the back door, ok?"

She doesn't ease up until we're in the back seat of the car. I had given the guy the address over the phone, and I take quite a bit of pleasure in watching Juniper try to figure out where we're headed. As we pull up to the boathouse along the lake, her eyes go huge. "Ty," she says, "What are we doing *here?*"

I hop out of the car and hold the door open for her. She lets me pull her hand as we walk to the door, where my man is waiting. I clap him on the back and slap some bills into his shirt pocket, saying, "Dude, thanks for setting this up for us. This is Juniper Jones, and she'd like to borrow a scull."

Juniper looks back and forth between us like she doesn't know what to say, which is likely a first for her. I give her a million-dollar grin, and tell Rick the boat guy, "Juniper had to miss training because she was out here for work. I'd really like it if she could stick with her workout before New Haven."

Rick looks skeptical as he pulls open the garage door. "You her coach?"

"Nah. Just a devoted fan, you might say." I pat his chest pocket again and say, "I'm a great supporter of the rowing community."

He blows air out of his cheeks and looks around, like he's not sure what to make of all this, but he walks Juniper over to a rack of boats and they pick one out that she likes. Rick walks with her to the dock, talking about her route and what she wants to do. He finally seems satisfied that she knows what she's talking about, and he comes to sit beside me as Juniper shoves off.

I settle in to watching her, mesmerized as always by her power and grace. Once she picks up speed, I remember that Rick is sitting next to me because I hear him whistle through his teeth. "Shit, dude. She's good." I nod, but it's nice to keep hearing in-the-know confirmation of what I can plainly see. "She's, like, really good," he tells me, and he pulls out his phone, opening up a timer app.

Rick tells me she's on par to place at nationals.

"Really? When's that race?"

He shakes his head. "Dude, it's like right now. Today. She'll have to wait for next year to compete there."

I exhale through my nose and watch as Juniper turns the boat and heads back toward us. I vow right there to make sure I'm watching *her* compete for the big cup next year instead of the other way around.

CHAPTER TWENTY-ONE

Juniper

This is the nicest thing someone has done for me since my dad adopted me, and I don't know what to say to him as we drive back to the hotel. It's too much. Sex is one thing, but this? Finding what makes me happiest and making it happen? First the filming and now this effort to make up for me missing my race. He knows me, and I realize how good it feels to be seen like this. And that makes it sting worse, because I can't be with him, and I hate that. He drapes an arm over my shoulders and plays with my hair, tucking and untucking it from behind my ear. I'm unsettled by how comfortable this feels, and know that I can't let anyone see. I whisper to him, "What if the driver puts something on social media?"

Ty drops a kiss on my cheek and pulls out his wallet. "I've got his business card, and I tipped him well not to. No worries, babe. I've been indiscreet with women before, you know."

I nod. "Yes, Tyrion, I do know. That's how you wound up with such a specific contract."

He laughs, but doesn't move away and eventually I let myself sink into his body like a warm blanket.

"I thought today was just a regular race you were missing, JJ. And that was bad enough. Why didn't you tell me you were missing nationals," he asks after a long silence. The truth is that I don't know. I never considered competing at nationals solo...and Derrick knew that I couldn't travel with the team, even as an alternate, because I had to be here with the Fury. I've been very disappointed that Murdo's recklessness cost me something I care about so deeply. I think about how I'll be flying back to a lonely apartment while the team will be out celebrating together, regardless of today's race outcome.

"I haven't finished deciding how I feel about it," I tell him by way of response. When he kisses me, turning my cheek up toward his mouth with his big hand, it's passionate and soft, pleading and apologetic all at once.

"Juniper," he whispers against my face. As the car pulls into the hotel drive, I stiffen. There are people everywhere, most with cameras. I leap from the car before it has a chance to come to a complete stop, willing Ty not to shout after me from the open window.

I manage to rush to his room and grab my bag. I can't do this. I can't risk being seen. I've been foolish. I scrawl *I'm sorry* on the hotel notepad on the desk in Ty's room and scurry out the front door without passing him in the hall. I grab a taxi straight for the airport, texting Matty that I won't be at the meeting and to send me any documents electronically. Matty can handle it, whatever it is. I spend the entire flight home trying to figure out how I'll deal with all the feelings I shouldn't have about Tyrion Stag, and then I push all that down inside and pull up other client contracts until I'm bleary-eyed from work.

Monday, Tim calls me into his office. He's worked out a deal for the baseball pitcher and can jump back in as point person with the NHL contracts. "Well that's shitty timing," I tell him, not bothering to hide the frustration in my voice.

"Juniper, I know this has been a lot to dump on you, especially when you are so new. That's partly why I wanted to talk with you today." He slides a folder across the desk, and I open it, raising an eyebrow at him in confusion. "I have a meeting with the Cavs," he says, grinning.

"The Cavs? Like in *Cleveland?*" He nods. "Tim, that's two hours away from here. How are we going to service those clients?"

He seems to brush aside my remarks, telling me what an opportunity this is for the firm and what an honor it should be to get considered for such an important contract. "We're going to have to really stretch ourselves to land this fish, Juniper." He asks me to help him prepare for a meeting with their executives next week.

I can't believe he's missing the point like this. Talk about no work-life balance. This is a nightmare. "I will help you prepare for the meeting, but I need you to know that I can't be involved in case work that takes me to Cleveland. As I said before, I value my free time more than a higher salary--"

"Juniper." Tim's voice is sharp. "This is the direction the company is heading. We are expanding. Rapidly. In no small part because of your work here this month! Now get the hell out of here and help me prepare the brief."

I raise both brows at him and stand. I move to walk out and he spins around in his desk chair. "One other thing."

Fuck. Does he know? He would have led with it if he knew I

was sleeping with his brother…right? I decide to stick with my irritated demeanor. "What now? Wooing a team in Tennessee perhaps?"

"Don't be a smart-ass, Juniper. That's not your style. No. The Fury's post-season gala is this Friday. Would you like to go as our representative? You did the bulk of the work, after all."

I consider this for a moment. A fancy party does sound nice, especially after the stress I've been under, but how can I go to a gala and simultaneously prepare for a meeting with a client I don't want our firm to take on? I open my mouth to decline, but Tim starts talking first.

"I'll have Donna send you the details. It's black tie. Bring a date." Tim walks me out of his office and closes the door. I hear him yell through the closed wood, "I want an update on the Cavs strategy tomorrow morning!"

A black tie formal and a major client pitch all in one week. Good thing I don't have a life outside of work. I pull my phone from my pocket and see a series of missed calls from Ty and two texts.

I wish u would talk 2 me
I miss u JJ

I lean against the wall and take some deep breaths. Nothing in my life is recognizable. College and law school were so orderly, if hectic. Rowing practice, studying, chill with Zack. I always knew what to expect. Not one thing has been predictable since that morning I walked in on my live-in boyfriend cheating on me. I don't know if I'm cut out for all this.

On my way back to my office, I pass the kitchen and see my friend Alice in there preparing lunch for the staff. She looks up and I guess she can tell my emotional state from my face, because she rushes into the hall. "Juniper, you look a mess," she says. I don't respond, but she tosses her chef coat onto a table. "Come on. Let's go downstairs for a coffee."

I can't tell her about the situation with Ty, but I am able to open up to Alice about my hesitation with this Cleveland deal and convince her to come shopping with me for a formal dress in one of the department stores downtown. "Alice, this isn't how I imagined my career in law," I tell her as we wander the aisles of gowns in the formalwear section.

"I always thought I'd be defending the disenfranchised…not bailing out superstar athletes caught with cocaine."

Alice laughs. "Technically, you didn't even do that. You're just following around hockey players and watching them get into fights!"

"Very funny. Do you think this one will make me look too tall?" I explained to her that I thought I'd ask Ben from work to be my date to the gala. He knows a lot of the players and NHL staff from being with the firm, and I'm pretty sure he's a safe date in terms of not trying anything romantic with me. His sister would have told me if he was into me that way. Ben is about the same height as me, though, so I'll have to wear flats or risk looking ridiculous at his side.

Alice urges me into a fitting room, and coos when I emerge in a champagne-colored, halter-top dress with a plunging v neckline. "Oh, Juniper! That looks amazing with your hair and your skin tone. That's the one!" The dress is sateen and shimmers when I move.

"You don't think the neckline is inappropriate for a work event?" I don't like how low it plunges. It's not my style, but Alice clucks her tongue at my concerns. "All right, then. Let's get out of here so I can finish that damn brief for the client I don't want so I have time to go to the damn   gala."

CHAPTER TWENTY-TWO
Ty

Usually I spend the off season pretty drunk, in the company of a revolving string of women whose names I forget as fast as I churn them out of my apartment. This year, none of that appeals to me. All I can think about is Juniper. I know she is feeling something for me, because she keeps running away from me when things get too intense. I know she's not used to this, but fuck. I'm not, either. I wish I could just go to the club, pick up some random woman and fuck her until I feel like myself again. But the thing is...I haven't been myself since I moved back home. I've been a different person. I actually like helping that rowing team with their publicity stuff. I like spending time with Juniper, damn it. All I've done for years is hang out with my brothers, hunt for tail, and play hockey. Now the hockey part is on hold for the off-season and my brothers are all busy with work.

I still show up at the arena every morning to work out for a few hours, but then I face long stretches of free time I'd rather be spending with my girl. If she'd ever let herself be my girl.

Juniper stopped responding to my flirty texts and doesn't pick up when I call. Something's up with her and I need to get her to tell me about it. Trying to distract myself, I've tightened every screw in my grandma's house, mowed every blade of her grass to perfection. Hell, I even hung out with my brother Thatcher at his damn glass studio in the heat of June, watching him make giant flower vases and shit. And all the while, I think of how I want to be taking Juniper to dinner, asking her about her training, watching her row. And then I remember I can't do any of those things because she's off limits.

The rowing teams are on hiatus after their big regatta, so I haven't even been hanging around the boat house. I had a few phone calls with Derrick about a television spot, but that's not even happening until fall. I think we've done just about all we're going to do with them in terms of my image strategy or whatever the hell Matty is calling it. The press loves me.

Coach is in a good mood now that we've won the Cup. I'm supposed to be living it up, but I just feel like I'm drifting.

After about a week of me sulking around, my grandma whacks me in the head with a newspaper while we're eating lunch.

"What the hell, Gram?"

"You're a mope, Tyrion Stag. What are you doing with yourself?"

"Jesus, that hurt. I'm trying to relax a bit is all." I try to go back to eating my sandwich, but Gram is relentless.

"Get out of here and go do something. Go to the library. Visit kids at a hospital. I don't want to see your mopey face back here today."

I decide to go for a long run and take Gram up on the idea to visit kids at the children's hospital. I spend hours there, giving each kid a photo op and signing everything they hand me. Their moms swoon and all the dads pat me on the back and ask when it's my turn for a day with the Cup. I feel good, but it doesn't last. After all that, I'm alone with my thoughts again. Only one thing feels right to me, and I decide I'm just going to go for it.

Before I can reconsider, I'm knocking on the door of Juniper's townhouse.

She answers and I watch her face drop in fear. "What are you doing here?" she hisses, pulling me inside and slamming the door. "Someone is going to recognize you, Ty. People use the bike path all the time."

I pull her into my arms and just inhale her scent. I haven't seen her in almost a week. Too long. "I just had to see you, Juniper." And then I claim her mouth with mine. I feel her struggling with her doubts, and then give in to wanting me.

She sighs, says my name like a whispered prayer. "Ty." It doesn't take long for me to strip her out of her work clothes, wrestle out of my jeans, and work our way over to the couch.

We don't say a word, but she grabs the condom from my jeans on the floor, rips it open with her teeth, and rolls it onto my shaft. I pull her onto my lap and she straddles my waist with those long, thick thighs of hers. I can't help but moan as she sinks home.

Juniper braces her hands on my chest and rides me like she's taking out all her anger at the world. It's fierce and it's fast and intense. I don't let her look away, keeping my eyes locked on hers while I knead her ass cheeks and drive up into her as she slams against me. "Yes, baby. Fuck me just like that." She finds the friction she needs and tilts her hips, bouncing up and down on my dick until her tits are shaking and I feel her clench around me. I let go right along with her.

This is what I want. I want to make love to this woman and

just melt into her. I think back to the hotel and how good I felt *after* we finished, when I just got to hold her and talk with her about life. She's collapsed against me on my lap now, and I just want to sit here with her until we grow old and creaky.

Eventually, she rolls off my lap and lies on her back on the couch with her legs sprawled across me. "Why Tyrion?" she says.

"Huh?"

"Why Tyrion and not Tyler or something? For Ty?"

"Oh." I get up to throw away the condom, and tell her, "My mom was really into reading *Game of Thrones* when she was pregnant with me. Then it became sort of a joke--I was the youngest, but I was always the biggest. I'd tell you I was the smartest, too, but we all know that's Tim." She laughs and I nestle in beside her, stroking her arm and just lavishing the chance to be close to her. I love that she's letting me in. "How come you're not on the pill, Juniper?"

She doesn't answer for a while, so long that I wonder if she fell asleep, but she finally explains that it just never felt like a good idea. "And in the end, Zack was cheating on me. Who knows what disease I might have caught if I'd been on the pill and stopped using condoms. I guess I'm nervous to trust anyone that much again." The thought of him betraying her like that makes me draw my hands into fists. I want to tell her she'd never have to worry about that with me, that she can always trust me to keep her safe, but the words don't seem to come to me. I realize some of the fan-girls I slept with might have had boyfriends or husbands. A wave of shame rolls over me at how I used to behave. Now that I've found someone, found Juniper, I realize what I was missing out on.

"I hate that that fucker abused your trust, Juniper," I breathe into her hair.

She turns her head to look up at me. "We can't keep doing this or I'll get fired."

"Juniper," I say, my voice serious, "I'm going to figure something out. I want to be with you, baby. For real with you."

She looks away and eventually starts to put her clothes back on. "Hey," I say, tugging on her arm. "You've got to stop running away from me when things get real."

She lets out a "humph," but I keep going. "I'm serious, Juniper. You've been avoiding me for a week since we made love at the hotel. I fucking miss you. Let's work on this thing together."

"There's nothing, Ty. There's no way out of this. You should leave."

I pull her back onto the couch beside me, half dressed. I don't give a fuck what she is wearing. Or preferably not wearing. "I'm. Not. Leaving." I punctuate each word with a kiss on her neck and shoulder. I feel her melt into me and I know, for a little at least, that I got her to forget about work shit and just be with me.

We turn on the television and just hang out until I realize I'm half starved. "You got any food, JJ?"

She wrinkles her brow and shakes her head. "I might have some protein bars…"

"Nah. I need a full meal. We'll have to order in."

I can see her hesitate about this, but there's nothing to be done. "I'm staying overnight, Junebug, so you'd better feed me something. I'll hide in the bedroom and you can answer the door for the delivery guy, ok?"

Except that when the food arrives, Juniper is in the shower, so it's me answering the door for a young kid in a Fury jersey. A fan. Of course. "Holy shit! Ty Stag!" the kid practically drops my food, which I grab from him before disaster strikes.

"In the flesh," I say, looking over my shoulder to make sure Juniper doesn't hear any of this. "I'll sign anything you want and snap a pic with you if you promise to forget my friend's address here. What do you say?"

The kid's jaw drops, so I grab his phone and snap a selfie of us together. Then I sign a receipt for him, scribbling his name from his nametag while he just stands there mute. I stuff an extra twenty in his fist and usher him out the door just as Juniper comes out of the bedroom with a towel wrapped around her head.

"You didn't answer the door, did you, Ty?" She looks worried.

"Never fear, babe. The kid had no idea who I was and I paid cash."

CHAPTER TWENTY-THREE
Juniper

In the morning, it's hard to go to the office. I woke up in bed entwined with Ty, showered with him, ate breakfast with him, and told him how much I hated working on this Cleveland briefing. It felt like a fantasy of how life could be if I were in a real relationship instead of unethically fucking my famous client. Then I had to leave him, sneak out of my own house like a fugitive while this man I care about so much slinked away in a hoodie like some sort of cat burglar.

He called Donna at work to set up a meeting with me for official business, but that doesn't brighten my day. I have to pretend like he's just a regular client, like he wasn't inside my body or listening to me bare my soul, talking about the loss of my dad and what that's meant for my life.

At lunch, when we're looking over his endorsement contracts, I notice that he's supposed to pose with the captain of the local women's hockey team for a promotional campaign. "We have a women's hockey team in Pittsburgh?" I never heard of them.

Ty shrugs. "I mean, it's not like they're the pros, but yeah. I've met some of them. They're nice."

We go over all his paperwork, but I can't get the women's hockey team out of my mind.

After he leaves, I call the team contact, Alicia, who turns out to be the team captain, coach, and business manager. They've got no funding, no legal representation, and are beyond thrilled for this advertising opportunity because they're going to put the funds toward their rink time. The whole team has day jobs, and everything they do is grass-roots, hard work, gritty. I explain to Alicia that I totally get it as a rower, and the experience gives me an idea.

For the rest of the week, I give only cursory attention to the

Cavs meeting and dive into my new theory for how I can enjoy my work more while helping Tim expand the firm. Alice actually has to drag me from my office on Friday to get ready for the gala. I can tell she's hiding something from me when she's helping me with my makeup in the women's room, but I don't press her about it, because then I'd be tempted to spill my own secrets. I try to just enjoy spending time with a friend, a real friend, and probably the first one I've made outside of rowing in years.

"Ugh," I tell her, sliding my dress over my head where Alice has topped off my smoothed hair with a glittering pin. "This freaking meeting with Cleveland."

She nods. "I just found out about it, actually. I mean that it's Monday and I have to cook for it. I wish Tim had given me more of a heads up. I'll be doing the menu the entire weekend."

I whip my head around. "You didn't know? Gosh, Alice. I feel like a jerk. I should have told you they were coming Monday! Want me to help you?"

She shakes her head, smiles a small smile. "Juniper, you look perfect. Go have an amazing time, and make sure to text me and describe the food in detail when you get home."

"Do they serve actual food at these things? I thought it would just be tiny bites with sauce drizzled in a pattern." I laugh, but promise to tell her all the details about the menu.

I had told Ben I'd meet him in the lobby of our office building, and I burst out laughing when I see him emerge from his office in his tux. "Working late like me, I see!" Apparently everyone in this place burns the candle at both ends. Not tonight. I'm determined to cut loose and enjoy myself.

"Juniper, you look radiant," he says, offering me an elbow. We share a cab over to the art museum. Along the way, Ben catches me up on Lisa's week, making me feel sheepish for not keeping in better touch, but he also tells me about the barista downstairs whom he's head over heels in love with, but too shy to make a move.

"Well now I know why you're always greeting me with a flat white," I say, laughing and really enjoying his revelation. I feel myself relax fully, knowing I can just be myself and not worry that he's going to make a move. We make a plan for him to slide her his number on Monday. The thought of his budding relationship takes my mind, of course, right back to work and my own personal tangle.

"Hey, Ben, I know we're supposed to relax tonight, but can I ask you something about work?"

"Sure. What's up?"

"Do you want this Cleveland thing to work out?"

He sighs. "Ah, I don't know, Juniper. I already feel like we're working pretty hard here. All of us! I mean, Tim's had you all over the country with the hockey team and I've had to step up with the NFL guys. Maybe Tim will hire new people if we land the Cavs?"

"Maybe." We pull up outside the building. Ben opens the door for me, lends me his elbow, and we joke about walking in on the red carpet. Of course, we aren't the celebrities the crowds are here to see.

Tonight is all about the Fury, and the press is here in force. Everyone is congratulating the team, the team staff. The atmosphere is so joyous.

I'm not sure why it didn't occur to me that I'd be walking into a hockey celebration where Tyrion Stag was sure to be a focal point. It just wasn't something I was thinking about when he was over the other day, and I haven't talked to him in a few days. It's not like he called me to ask if I'd be here, either. But the moment Ben and I walk into the atrium I feel his gaze upon me, dark and furious as Ben places a hand on my waist to usher me toward the bar.

"I feel like an idiot," I tell Ben as we wait for a drink. "I didn't stop to think that I'd be seeing the players tonight."

He laughs. "Why do you think I was so eager to say yes when you invited me? I gave up a good night to stare at my coffee gal so I can brush shoulders with the Fury! I love these guys."

He orders us each a drink, telling me how he's taking the liberty to go full fan-geek tonight. One of the guys walks up to us then, and Ben starts tugging on my elbow. It's Hayden Murphy, one of the guys I had to bail out for public urination.

Murphy smiles and hugs me, casually. "Juniper! Glad you could join us!"

"Hayden. Glad you stayed out of trouble so I could be here." I punch his arm playfully. "This is my colleague Ben. He's a big fan." I mouth "huge" and Hayden laughs. The guys take a selfie and start to talk about the last game.

When Hayden excuses himself, Ben pulls me into an excited hug and shows me the pictures. He's so excited I can't help but smile and lean into his hug. "Just don't let Tim know you're so star struck for the clients, Ben!"

"Never, Juniper. I'm all game face at work. Game face and golf puns."

He starts to chatter about the other Fury players here and my mind wanders as I sip my mojito.

Suddenly I feel my phone start to vibrate in my clutch. Repeatedly. A peek inside reveals a string of texts from Ty.

What the duck r u doing here?
Who is that asshole w u?

Why is he touching u, Juniper?

My face flushes, and I quickly zip my bag as Ben looks at me, concerned. "Everything ok?"

"It's fine. I just forgot to tell Ty that I was coming here to represent Stag Law." I gesture across the room, where Ty is still smoldering amongst a group of his teammates. Ben smiles and waves, but I know Ty doesn't know who he is. Why would he bother to remember some other random lawyer from his brother's firm? I'm the only one who has been traveling with them, joking around on their flights, bailing them out when groups of them get a little rowdy at the strip clubs. Ty shoots a look at Ben that would melt ice, and I can't decide if I should go over and try to calm him down.

Ben and I make our way toward the executives we are supposed to be thanking and get busy with the small talk and sucking up portion of our evening. I finish complimenting the team owner on his decision to sign Ty before playoffs as my phone begins to vibrate again. I'm able to glance at the new text, which reads **meet me in the stairwell.**

Now, JJ.

I glance around, but don't see Ty. "Would you excuse me," I say to Ben and the gang of suits. "I have a client with an urgent need I have to address." I walk away to the sound of them admiring my dedication as a lawyer and I hear Ben steering the conversation back to the playoff game where I intervened on Ty's behalf.

When I enter the stairwell, it's eerily silent. I see Ty standing down a level, staring at me. I've never seen him look like this before. I can feel his intense mix of emotions from ten feet above him. "Ty," I start, but as I approach him he pulls me in to a rough kiss. I pull back my head. "Are you drunk?"

"Who is that guy, Juniper?" I can smell the whiskey on him, but can tell that while he's been drinking, he's not drunk. He's angry and jealous.

"It's Ben. From the firm, Ty. A colleague. He got me this job with your brother and--"

"You're mine, Juniper. Don't you know that?" His voice is barely above a whisper as he boxes me in with his arms against the wall. "I should be able to tell Murphy to keep his filthy hands off you, too, but I fucking can't." I feel the heat of his body as he presses against me, and I want him. I know I shouldn't feel a thrill that I've stirred this emotion in him, that the thought of me here with another man has made him react this way. And yet I've never been more turned on in my life. I want so very badly to be his, in every way.

"I can't be yours, Tyrion." I fight back a tear. "I can't."

But then he's kissing me again and I respond. I need him, and

I kiss him with all my power, burying my fingers in his unruly mane, pulling his face into mine as he crushes my lips with his need. I gasp for breath when he breaks the kiss and stares into my eyes. "You're mine," he says again. I nod. He hisses, "I want you," and I nod again.

"I need you, Ty," I say, and then I yelp. He spins me around so I'm facing the wall and I feel him inching up my gown. I drop my forehead against the cool concrete blocks in the stairwell as Ty slides down my panties.

He runs his fingers down each of my calves slowly as he pulls the panties off, then stands. I hear him pull down his zipper, and I gasp when I feel the smooth, bare tip of his cock nudging me open.

"Ty!   Don't   you   have   a   condom?"

CHAPTER TWENTY-FOUR

Ty

"I need you so much, Juniper." I start kissing her neck, tucking that smooth, chestnut hair behind her ear. "I need you, now, with nothing between us."

"Oh god, Ty. I trust you. I trust you. But you have to pull out." She looks over her shoulder at me and I nod. She tilts her hips back, opening herself a little more for me to slide in. I've never been with a woman like this before, bare. Just me and her. "Jesus Christ, this feels so good, Juniper." Her pussy glides against my cock, the warm honey of her arousal coating us both as I slide in and out.

"There's nobody but you for me," I tell her, pistoning into her body, not caring who comes into the stairwell at this moment. Nothing exists except the warm, moist heat of Juniper Jones swallowing me body and soul. "Who makes you come, baby?"

She doesn't answer, just moans as I pick up the pace and reach around to massage that magical place that brings her over the edge. Desperate, she rocks her hips against my fingers. I pull back my hand. "Say it, Juniper. Who makes you come?"

"Christ, Ty. You do. Only you. Please." And at that, I press a knuckle against her clit in the way I know drives her wild. I feel her pussy contracting against my cock inside her as she comes.

"You make me cum so hard, Juniper," I groan, slamming into her once, twice more before I pull out. I cum right on her back, hot jets spraying out of me, marking her as mine. I feel savage and raw, and I lean my head against her shoulder, both of us breathing heavy. I massage her shoulders and start to ease her gown back down, but I don't wipe up the mess. I just kiss every inch of her I can reach. As I zip my fly, I think about her going back up to that party with my cum dripping out of her dress. The caveman in me rears up again and I remember the jealousy that brought me into this stairwell. "Juniper."

She turns to look at me, but neither of us says anything. What is there to say after what we just did? It was hot and intimate and primal. I stoop down and pocket her panties, which draws a short laugh from her. She smooths out her hair and opens her mouth to say something when I hear the door to the stairwell open above me. Juniper gasps and we look up to see Matty standing on the landing.

I lean back against the wall and don't say anything. Juniper walks up the stairs and past Matty, eyes wide, and goes back out to the party.

He starts to walk down the stairs after the door shuts and he stands next to me on the landing. "How long have you been fucking her, Stag?"

"It's not like that, Matty."

He holds a hand up to stop me. "Don't pull that shit with me, Ty. How long?"

I exhale. *Fuck it,* I decide. "Since the day I met her," I tell him. "I'm in love with her, Matty."

This makes his jaw drop. I didn't know I was going to say that, but once it falls out of my mouth I know it's true. I fucking love that woman. I've rendered him speechless, and that's saying something for a sports agent. He's seen a lot of shit in his day. "You *love* her? You?" I nod. He whistles. "Well that's unexpected. I thought you were just screwing her to get back at your brother or something."

"Come on, man. I can screw anyone I want. I don't need to do my brother dirty that way."

"All right, all right." He leans against the wall. "She the one who gave you the bloody nose at the DMV?"

I nod, and he laughs. "I ought to take self-defense lessons from her. Seems like she knows what she's doing."

He has no fucking idea how strong my girl is, but I'm not about to go into all that right now.

"This entire stairwell reeks of sex, Ty. You know that, right?" I nod. He claps me on the back. "Let's get back up there and we'll figure something out."

By the time I get back to the party, Juniper is gone. I call her, but she doesn't answer. **At least let me know u got home safe,** I text her, but I don't even see that she reads my message. That Ben fucker is gone, so I'm hoping he got her home. Every fucking time, that woman runs out when shit gets intense. I sigh and head for home, promising myself I'll find her in the morning.

Matty calls me before dawn. I'm half hungover, slumped sideways across my bed and I only reached over to pick up the phone because I thought it'd be Juniper. "We've got a problem, buddy. Pull up TMZ. I'll wait." I roll sideways and pull up the website on my phone. I see pictures of myself coming out of Juniper's townhouse--grainy, far-off shots of me kissing her goodbye, walking away toward my car. The headline reads LUSTING FOR LAWYER and there's some puff piece bullshit about how I'm boning my lawyer in secret.

"That fucking delivery guy," I say to Matty. "I tipped him, gave him an autograph, and took a damn selfie with him and he still ratted me out to the paparazzi. How did they find out Juniper's name?"

Matty prattles on about data aggregate sites and how much information is public if you feel motivated to search. I can feel my blood start to boil as fast as the whiskey hangover sends my head throbbing.

"Look, what are the chances that your brother is aware of this?"

I wait for a beat and say, "Ordinarily, I think he'd be on top of this shit immediately. But I know he meets with the Cavs on Monday and I think he's holed up with his secret girlfriend preparing all weekend."

"Your brother has a girlfriend, too?"

"Some chick my grandma knows from when we were growing up," I tell him. "She's a muffin chef. Or something. He doesn't think we know, but he's been seeing her on the sly for weeks."

"All right, Ty. Give me until Monday and I'll figure something out. Luckily this doesn't seem too scandalous and I don't think it'll stick much to the top of the gossip sites. You better hope one of your teammates pees in the Stanley Cup or something this weekend."

CHAPTER TWENTY-FIVE
Juniper

I can't bear to stay at the gala after Matty nearly caught us in the hallway. What happened with Ty was too intense for me to just go back up there and make small talk. I tell Ben and the execs I need to focus on a client, remind everyone how much time I spend bailing the Fury out of the drunk tank, and I leave to high fives and martini salutes. Ben and I share a cab back to Stag Law and work on the Cavs presentation for awhile.

"I'm sorry I took you from your celebrity hockey party," I say.

He shrugs. "Plenty more where that came from. What do you think about these numbers for workers comp claims?" We work for a few more hours and eventually I take a cab home, worn out. I feel empty inside and barely sleep.

When I finally drift off around dawn, I wake to the sound of my phone buzzing on the nightstand. Another set of texts from Ty.

U up? Need 2 talk

Also this. He sent a link to a series of studies about birth control and performance in female athletes. Something about fewer knee injuries.

I roll my eyes and send back, **ok ok I get it. You like it bareback.** I flush thinking about what happened between us last night. How raw his want for me was and how much I responded to him. I was out of my mind with passion. It was a totally new level for me, even with Ty.

Just looking out for ur rowing, babe. Call me, though. Important.

Is this a thing I do now? Call up Ty and let him call me babe over text message? I sigh and dial his number. He answers on the first ring, like he's sitting there waiting for me to call. "Good morning, gorgeous. Did you shower yet?"

"What? Why?"

"Just wondering if you've still got me all over your beautiful backside."

"Jesus, Ty. You're disgusting. You're lucky you didn't stain my gown." I blush again, remembering his finale in the stairwell.

"I would buy you a new one. It was worth it. Anyway, listen. Something happened."

I remember that Matty had walked into the stairwell just after we had finished fucking, but I feel pretty sure he hadn't seen anything definitive. "What?" My voice is hesitant, but doesn't shake as much as my hands.

"I mean, you know Matty knows. But he's not the problem."

"What are you talking about, Ty?"

"We're on TMZ."

I feel like my insides are turning out. I start to hyperventilate. *I'm going to lose my job and I'm going to get disbarred.* "Juniper!" I realize Ty must have been calling out to me.

"I'm here. What are we going to do? There's going to be a fucking ethics review, Ty."

"We're going to talk with Tim. Matty says he thinks it'll be ok. Listen, since everyone knows about us anyway, do you want to come have breakfast with me and my grandma? She can meet you as my girlfriend."

"Ty, this is all really fast for me. I don't share your confidence that Tim is going to be ok with this and--"

"Just come over for pancakes. Tim is holed up with Alice getting ready for the Cavs on Monday. I promise he's not looking at the celebrity gossip."

I snort. Tim is a maniac about that contract with Cleveland. I want to tell Ty that I need to be working on it, too, but I don't want that client. I don't want to work this weekend. I want to go eat pancakes with my boyfriend and his grandmother, and I start crying into the phone from all the stress of the whole situation.

"Hey, Junebug. Hey. Don't shut me out this time. Don't run away from me. Do you want me to come get you? Let me take care of you today."

When he talks to me, his voice as smooth as maple syrup, I feel safe. He makes me think it can somehow all be ok. That I can be a person who eats weekend pancakes with my lover and his grandma. Some sort of fantasy orphan chicks don't even dare to utter out loud. And yet he's right there on the other end of the phone assuring me it's all real. "No, I'll be ok," I sniffle. "When should I come over?"

"I smell bacon, Junebug. You better hurry before I eat it all."

A half hour later, I find myself parked outside the Stag family home, still on the verge of hyperventilating. As I ring the doorbell, I realize I shouldn't be officially meeting his grandmother wearing sweatpants. Why didn't I stop to change? Or buy flowers? The door opens.

"Juniper! Dear! Come inside." Anna Stag ushers me into the house before I can apologize for my informality. "When Tyrion told me he wanted to introduce me to the woman who makes him mopey, I was hoping it would be you!"

"Mopey?" *Does everyone in this family speak in code,* I wonder. She pulls me into the kitchen and hands me a mug of coffee, hollering for Ty to come down and greet his "own damn girlfriend."

He pulls me in for a kiss and I stiffen instinctively, forgetting that I'm here to discuss a plan to go public with our relationship. He rubs my back and I relax into his arm, clutching the caffeinated brew. Once I finish the coffee, I feel like I can concentrate enough to ask questions. "Did you say Tim was with Alice this weekend? Why would they be together preparing for the meeting? Unless..."

Mrs. Stag smiles as she flips pancakes into the air. Ty nods. "Oh, big time. He thinks we don't know, but Gram saw him over at her house a bunch of times playing with her nephews."

"I can't..." I try to imagine my stern boss playing with children and come up at a loss. "That sounds so unlike him. But you know, Alice has been on the verge of telling me something for a month now. Huh. Tim and Alice."

"Try these, dear," Mrs. Stag says, sliding me a plate of pancakes. "I know Tyrion said you worry about your food, too, so I added flax and buckwheat to these."

I taste a forkful of the pancakes, and I melt into my stool at the counter. "These are amazing, Mrs. Stag."

She pats my hand. "You should have been calling me Anna a long time ago, dear. And I got these recipe ideas from Alice."

As I eat, Ty and his grandma talk about how they think we should use Tim's secret relationship to our advantage. I'm not really comfortable with the idea of capitalizing on something like this, but Ty says we're not going to blackmail him. "No way, JJ. I'm going to explain that I couldn't help but fall for you, like he couldn't help but fall in love with Alice. Like a--what's that called, Gram?"

"It's an analogy, dear," she says, smiling.

I shake my head. "I think you're both being naive about this." I can't stop eating the delicious pancakes and Ty's grandma slides me a plate of bacon. "But I do think you're right that he won't notice this happened until at least after the meeting on Monday."

Ty and his grandmother both start to talk about how much they hate the idea of him expanding the firm too fast, too big. Ty gets especially angry when I mention that Tim implied I might have to do some travel to service the new clients if we land the deal. I sit in the kitchen with them for hours, talking and eating, until I realize I've nearly missed my morning opportunity to row before all the beer cruise boaters get reckless on the river. I excuse myself to go train, and allow myself to savor the comfortable, familiar feeling of kissing Ty by my car before driving away. *Could this be my future,* I wonder. It feels too good to be true.

I stay up late Sunday preparing for Monday's meeting, and enter it with a heavy heart. I don't want it to be successful, and yet I can't allow myself to perform poorly on purpose. The morning of, I climb into my best power suit, complete with heels. I like to look as tall as possible when I'm presenting for a crowd. I am at eye level with the suits when we shake hands in the hall at work. Tim seems delighted. I feel distracted throughout the budget presentation and when Tim takes the lead to discuss numbers, individual athlete contracts, and injury clauses, I notice that Alice looks practically grey as she passes out trays of food in the conference room.

I try to catch her attention to ask if she's ok, when I see her start to faint. Then, all hell breaks loose at the office.

CHAPTER TWENTY-SIX
Ty

"Thatcher, pick up the damn phone." I yell into his voicemail as I barrel down the highway toward his studio. "Fuck!" When he doesn't answer I keep driving. To hell with him if he has some woman squirreled away in his studio today. I knew something was wrong when I didn't hear from Tim or Juniper on Monday after their meeting, and then she called me this morning with the news. I screech to a halt in the gravel lot outside Stag Glass and throw open the door.

My brother is bent over his workbench, blaring music and banging away at some red-hot piece of molten glass. I shut off his radio, but don't get too close because I don't want that fucker to burn me. "Thatcher. We have a problem, man."

He frowns, plunges his work into a bucket of water, and raises his eyebrows--my permission to explain myself. "Juniper just called."

"Your lawyer?"

I wave away that question. "Listen, she said Alice fainted during their big meeting at the law firm and cut her head. Tim rode with her to the hospital and then went insane, holed himself up in his office, and just rushed out of there all bloody and wild-eyed."

Thatcher just stares at me.

"Dude, Tim has been fucking Alice."

"Our brother Tim? Mr. stern Stag? And one of his *employees*?"

I nod. "I know, man, but he's freaking out. Apparently he drove over to Alice's house spewing some insane scheme. Juniper said he was holed up in his office ever since he got back, muttering."

Thatcher scratches his beard, thinking. "He told me he was banging some chick without a condom. A few weeks ago. He said she drove him to distraction." Thatcher shrugs. "Where is he now?"

"Let's go, man, he's probably over at the Peterson house

causing a scene."

We drive in search of our brother and I fill Thatcher in on my TMZ situation. Thatcher laughs when I tell him I'd been planning to use Tim's distraction at work as a screen to convince him it's cool that Juniper and I are together. "His situation sure trumps yours, baby bro."

I grit my teeth and head to our neighborhood, where the Petersons live just a few streets away from me and Gram.

Only Tim isn't at the Peterson house anymore.

When we pull up, Alice's brothers are sitting on the porch with a metal baseball bat. Thatcher laughs. "This doesn't look great, Ty."

I see Tim's car parked half in the street, blocking their driveway. "Thatch, let's go up there together."

"I'm not going anywhere near this shit-show, baby brother," he says, tugging on his damn beard. "Listen, you go talk to them and tell them you'll move Tim's car."

I shake my head at my brother and climb out of my Tesla. "Hey, Petersons," I call, walking toward them with my hands up. "We just came to find our brother. We don't want to cause any trouble here."

One of the Peterson brothers stands up. The one with the bat. I can handle a bat. "It's me, Ty Stag. You guys went to school with my brothers?"

"You mean your crazy ass brother who knocked up our sister and showed up here trying to kidnap her?"

"What?"

"You heard me, Stag. Get the fuck out of here. Move that fucking car of his while you're at it."

I freeze in my tracks. I feel my face contorting. Did he say pregnant? My brother Tim got his girlfriend pregnant? "Hey, guys, what do you say you put the bat down and I sign some autographs for the kids and you tell me exactly what my dickhead brother did so I can make amends."

Thatcher and I park Tim's car at Gram's house and walk the neighborhood, until we eventually find him in the park. He's slumped over by the fountain looking like he's been in a fight with Satan himself. We sit on either side of him and pat his leg, which is bro-speak for "everything is going to be ok, dude."

I give him an exaggerated sniff. He's obviously been wearing the same clothes for a few days. I have never seen him disheveled like this, even when he was cramming for law school exams. "Bro, I hate to tell you this, but your shirt is untucked," I say. Thatcher cracks up and starts plucking blades of grass off the shoulders of Tim's suit.

Tim has been our rock for over ten years. Nobody asks to be responsible for their snot-nosed brothers, but Tim stepped up as soon as it was obvious our dad wasn't going to be around to parent us. I realize, looking at him falling apart like this, that it's all been really one-way. Even once we became adults, Thatcher and I never reached out to him or offered any sort of support. "Tim, you know you can talk to me about stuff, right? I mean...shit. I'm here for you no matter what. God knows you've been there for me." Thatcher nods.

"We're going to be amazing uncles," I say. "And from the looks of things, Baby Stag's got some other uncles who'll look out for him, too."

Thatcher lets out a huff, muttering about a shotgun wedding until I punch him in the shoulder. I wish I were better at talking about this stuff. Tim's still staring off into space, blood on his shirt, stubble on his face for the first time I've ever seen. "All those times you bailed me out, talked to teachers when I got in fights, made sure I was allowed to stay in school. Tim, you've been a dad to me for a long time, bro. You've been *our* dad. You're already good at this, is what I'm trying to say."

He looks over at me then, like he finally hears me. His eyes are all watery, and I choke up. Thatcher pipes in, saying, "It's true, Tim-bo. You're already good at being everybody's dad." Tim closes his eyes and his body seems to relax a bit more.

"Come on," I say, giving him a lift to his feet. "Let's get you home before Alice's brothers come after us with their hunting rifle."

CHAPTER TWENTY-SEVEN

Juniper

Things have been crazy at work since Alice passed out. As soon as we got her off in the ambulance, I snapped into action mode with the executives from the Cavs. I managed to spin Tim's panicked departure into a description of him as a devoted and dedicated leader, which is all true. But everything about the presentation sat wrong with me.

Since I came here, I compromised almost everything that's important to me. I'm sleeping with a client, which is unethical no matter how strong my feelings might have grown for Ty. I'm slacking on my rowing, I took a leave from the women's rowing team, I missed watching tryouts for nationals...there is almost nothing left I recognize about myself.

While I try to settle my mind, there's nothing I can think to do other than escape to the boathouse. I reach for the phone to call Lisa in Boston, but saying all this stuff out loud feels too overwhelming. I can't really call Alice, because she's got enough going on with her drama. And Ty. I just can't call him right now, either. Everything is a mess.

I've got nothing on my plate at work right now anyhow. All my NHL clients are behaving themselves and I'm pretty sure I unwittingly bagged the Cavs contract. Might as well take to the river while I still can.

I hoist my scull out of the garage, running my hand along the hull. I get her onto the water and take my time adjusting my shoes once I'm seated inside. She's in fantastic shape despite her neglect of late, and as I shove off the dock, I feel like I'm slipping back into my own skin for the first time in a few weeks.

I have no plan in mind, but I just need to row. I head up river toward the dam, the island passing by my periphery in a blur of green leaves. I see people standing along the shore sometimes, but I don't want to break form to wave back at them. I've got too much negative energy to burn off.

Later--I'm not even sure how long I was out, to be honest--I pull up to the dock and am surprised to see Derrick waiting there. He helps me out of my boat and remains quiet while we get everything put away. I start to chug from my water bottle as he leans on the wall and says, "So. Juniper."

I just raise my eyebrows but keep drinking. I'm exhausted. I was really going hard there at the end. Derrick isn't usually around in the afternoon since he coaches all morning. "I was up filing some paperwork in the boathouse office and I saw you heading up river," he says. "I came out on the deck to watch, and then I couldn't look away." I'm not really sure what to say to him, so I fidget while I wait for him to continue. I still feel bad about pulling out of the women's team with so little notice.

"Juniper, you know you're the best rower I've ever seen come through here. You have to know that."

My jaw just drops open, and I can feel my eyes go wide. *The best ever?* Derrick strokes his chin, thinking, and then says, "Putting you in the middle of an 8-seat boat would be wasting your talents. I know you missed qualifiers for nationals--hear me out!" I am about to interject something about work, but I close my lips. "I made a call. The staff for the women's national team is willing to come to New Haven this weekend and whatever time you get for the singles races there can qualify you for a spot on the Olympic team, Juniper."

"Are you serious, Derrick? The Olympics? Quit messing around with me." I figure he must be pissed that I ditched his team. I know they didn't do well last weekend. But this seems a bit far-fetched. The Olympics! I haven't even been training carefully.

"Juniper! Your dad was an Olympic rower. Your form is textbook perfect when you're not focused on it. Your stamina is unparalleled and if you can put out the kind of speed I just saw while navigating around coal barges, I'm pretty sure you're going to do fine on the water in Tokyo!"

I start walking away from him, toward my townhouse. I'm not even sure why I'm so angry. His words bring up all sorts of feelings about my childhood, about my dad. I row to drown out the anger inside, to keep me focused on work. I'm not trying to be some Olympian. "Juniper! Wait up." Derrick chases me down, doesn't back away when I freak out. This surprises me, too. I'm just not used to people sticking around with me when shit gets hard. He says, "I'd like to help you train...you know, after you qualify next weekend."

"You're serious about all this? Me? I just...I blend in better in the team boat, Derrick. I've never raced solo before."

Derrick breaks into a grin. "Then we are all in for a fucking treat this weekend, Juniper Jones. I'm serious as a heart attack. Go home and start getting your shit ready for New Haven this weekend. We leave Friday   at   7am."

CHAPTER TWENTY-EIGHT
Ty

Juniper isn't answering her phone and when I swing by her townhouse, it doesn't seem like she is home ignoring me, either. This is the longest I've gone without talking to her since...well, ever. I spent a lot of time with Tim this week talking him through all his anxiety about Alice and the pregnancy. And then I spent a ton of time trying to find Juniper and not succeeding.

As my Gram would say, I've been a mope. I did the whole circuit, everything I'm supposed to do. Nothing is right without Juniper. All of it feels empty and shallow. There is nothing my trainer can do to work me hard enough to forget how empty I'm feeling without the sound of her voice.

I have no idea why she's avoiding me since she called to tell me the news about Tim and Alice, but I can only assume something happened at work with Tim going off the rails. And so I do the thing she told me not to do: I drive downtown and barge into her office.

And she's not there. Her laptop isn't on the desk, her purse isn't hanging on the door. *What the fuck?* She's not at home and she's not at work? Something isn't right here. I start to panic that she told my brother about us and he fired her already. But where would she have gone even if that happened?

Raking my fingers through my hair, I can't even think straight. I stomp down the hall and past Donna, right into my brother's corner office.

He's sitting behind his desk, his chair turned so he's staring out the window at the river. I can't tell if he's still panicking, or just pensive, or what. "Tim, we need to talk, brother."

He doesn't turn around. I see him sigh. "What's going on now, Ty? Please tell me how I have fucked up your life, too. Maybe take a number, though. The list is getting long."

I sit down in one of the chairs at his desk. It's too small for

94

me. "Jesus, Tim, if you're going to represent athletes, you need to get some bigger fucking chairs in your office."

He swivels around at that and sees me trying to wedge myself out from between the unforgiving arm rests. I slump over to the couch instead. "I just need to say that you can't fire Juniper."

"Fire her? Why would I do that?"

Oh. So he doesn't know after all. Then where the fuck is she? I'm starting to try to piece together where she might be when Tim presses me for more. "Ty, why would I fire her? Why would you storm in here worried that I'd fire Juniper Jones?"

I clear my throat uncomfortably, and say, "Well, I can't find her, so I assumed you fired her."

"Why would you be looking for her? All your business is settled for the next few months at least. She's at some damn boat race. Left this morning. Wait a minute--"

His eyes spark and he stands up, starts pacing. "She called *you* to tell you about Alice."

"Yeah, because she was worried about you. With reason!"

"No. This is different." He squints at me. "I can't fucking believe you, Ty. You're sleeping with her."

I pause a second too long, and Tim continues railing into me. "You can't leave one thing alone without dipping your dick in it, can you? Not my study group in law school. Not the fucking cheerleaders from the high school hockey team. And not my best employee. I really don't need this right now from you."

"Tim, it's not like that."

"Get the hell out of my office."

"No way, man. Not until you talk to me about this."

"This is seriously the last thing I need right now when I'm trying to figure out how to support a fucking family now with Alice and Juniper both telling me I'm an idiot. Jesus, I just passed on the Cleveland deal, Ty. Do you know how that makes me look? I went after them and then told them no thank you and--"

"Tim, I'm in love with her."

"What?"

"Juniper. I'm not just sleeping with her. I'm in love with her. I want to be with her. Like, forever. I think."

"What are you even talking about?"

"I'm telling you I didn't just come into your office and fuck your employees to be an asshole like when I was younger. I met Juniper before she started here. And I'm in love with her."

"She'd been sleeping with you and still took you on as a client? Jesus Christ. This is an ethics nightmare. Does your agent know about this?"

"I mean, she didn't know who I was then...it's just...it's complicated."

"You're damn right it's complicated, Tyrion! God, get out of here so I can get to work trying to fix this."

"You of all people should know about falling in love with someone you maybe shouldn't. Or was that not you rutting on the conference table in the hockey arena with your corporate chef?"

"You need to shut your mouth and get out of here, brother."

"I saw the damn security footage, Tim. So don't tell me you don't know what it's like to get carried away. And now you and Alice are having a baby. And Juniper and I are in love." I stand up and start walking toward him, not sure what I'm going to do but not feeling particularly civil. It's been awhile since we Stag brothers had a brawl.

"You're so in love you didn't know she was off competing in a boat race this weekend? Spare me, Ty."

I freeze. He's right about that. Why didn't she tell me she was going to race? I sigh, take a deep breath, and continue. "Look, just reassign me to Ben or whatever his name is. Can you do that? And don't fire Juniper?"

He starts laughing, but it's a sort of crazed laugh. "I can't fire her. She's a fucking genius. She could be fucking my entire client list and I couldn't fire her. I wonder if she knows that..."

Tim starts muttering something about return on investment, but I stopped listening to him after he said he couldn't fire my girl. I don't even say goodbye, but I brush past him and head down the hall. I have to figure out where the hell she went.

Suddenly, I remember that Ben guy has a sister who rows. Juniper knew her from Boston. I bet he knows where she is this weekend. But where the hell will I find *him?* I'm stomping around like an idiot when I stumble across the kitchen. "Alice!"

She screams and drops a pan of food. "Oh shit, Alice, I'm sorry I scared you. Are you ok?" I rush over and help her pick everything up. "I'm really sorry."

"Ty, it's ok. You just startled me."

"Hey, so, can I say congratulations? About growing my niece or nephew in there?"

Her face lightens up and I can tell not too many people have been happy for her about this. She throws her arms around me--as much as she can. Alice is a really tiny person--and thanks me.

"Oh come on, Alice. Don't thank me--of course I'm excited about a baby. Anything you need, you let me know. Even if that's just to beat some sense into my brother." I pop one of the dropped pastries into my mouth, and of course it tastes amazing. She smiles at me. "Hey, you wouldn't know where Juniper is this weekend, would you?"

Alice looks puzzled. "She didn't tell you?" I shake my head. "She's at the regatta in New Haven."

"New Haven! I remember that that was her upcoming race. Awesome."

"But there's more! The rowing coach guy saw her training earlier this week."

I listen as Alice tells me everything about Juniper's big opportunity. I can't fucking believe she shut me out from this, but I'm not missing it. I'm going to support her no matter what, in person. I rush out of the Stag Law building to catch the first flight I can find.

CHAPTER TWENTY-NINE
Juniper

"All right, ladies, I want all of you in bed by 9," Derrick says as he slides his credit card to the server at the restaurant. "Tomorrow is a big day for some of us, and a huge day for Juniper."

I blush immediately and look down as he draws attention to the fact that I'm here as a separate entity. A sort of tag along with the team. "Cheers to that," says Ashley, one of the rowers from the team boat. The women on either side of me clap me on the shoulders. They wish me luck. I'm stunned by their support for me, which I don't feel like I've earned, but all they care about is that the Pittsburgh team gets mentioned when they put out the list of rowers for Tokyo. "Our city is going to be known for producing Olympic-caliber crew," Ashley says, winking.

We all walk back to our hotel rooms and start our pre-race rituals. I'm not even sure what to do for mine, since I'm not going to be on a team tomorrow. I've got my uniform laid out, my sunglasses and sunscreen. We're all checked in at the docks already. There's not much to do but sleep and show up at this point.

Nobody chats much as we get ready for bed. There's one thing you can count on with rowers, and that's an eager, early bedtime. Years of getting up at 5am means we're all ready for sleep practically as soon as it gets dark, if not before.

I lie in my bed and think about the past week, about the Stag brothers. When I went to talk with Tim about taking off on Friday for the race, I reiterated that I wouldn't consider traveling to support the Cleveland account. He surprised me by telling me he decided not to go after that client. I know he's worried about the reputation of the firm, since he wooed them hard core, but I'm pretty sure it'll be ok in the end. Ultimately it's better not to expand too rapidly, too wide.

While I was in his office, I talked to him about my idea about the women's hockey team from Ty's promo shoot. Tim was surprised to learn about all the pay inequities with women's sports. A huge smile spreads across my face as I think about our new agreement. I convinced Tim to let me represent the women's hockey team pro bono in their case seeking equal treatment. Tim had no idea these women weren't even offered disability insurance to compete for our country, let alone were being crammed in coach when they flew to away games. The US men's team gets private jets! The next winter Olympics, I vowed to Tim that I'd make sure our national women's teams received equal funding to represent our country. "Think of the publicity opportunities for Stag Law surrounding the Olympics," I'd told him. A few hours later, Tim had emailed me to ask about women's basketball and soon, we had mapped out a plan of Title IX opportunities that would keep me busy for the next few years.

Of course, these cases will never bring in a fraction of the income even something simple like Ty's endorsement contracts can swing, but I told Tim that profit can't always be the bottom line. I got really fired up, telling him how much diversity and inclusion matters to communities, and how proud I would be to help shepherd Stag Law through these endeavors. Pittsburgh and Stag Law will be famous for defending women's rights and athletic equality. I get chills just thinking about it.

I headed off to Connecticut today feeling confident in my work at least. I decide to put off thinking about Ty until I have more energy to focus. I need to make sure I get enough rest so I can perform well, make it worth it for the national team staff to have traveled here for my own Olympic dreams. I drift off to sleep thinking about the rhythm of the oars, the pull of the current, and the slip of my boat in the water.

CHAPTER THIRTY
Ty

A few minutes with Google is all I need to find my way to the regatta early Saturday morning. According to the schedule, Juniper's race starts around 8am, but I want to get there early enough to see if I can find her coach and find the best place to watch.

Some of the women milling around start calling my name, and I recognize them from the Pittsburgh team. "Ty! You made it up here to watch us! That's so nice of you." The short girl named Tina grabs my arm and pulls me to the Pittsburgh team. I immediately relax as I head over to them and get the scoop.

Apparently Juniper is in the zone getting ready for her race, and I'm not going to mess with that, so they show me where I can sit in the bleachers near the finish area. I settle in with them, waiting for her heat. I can see the officials and the men with clipboards on the floating dock, and I know those are the guys determining Juniper's rowing future.

There are four lanes set up for the race, and I see four women getting their boats set up way up river. Ashley hands me binoculars and points out Derrick at the start area. He's hanging onto the ball on Juniper's bow, I guess so her boat doesn't drift over the start line. I try to fight back my jealousy that it's not me there whispering encouragement to her before the race. I try not to remember that she didn't even call me before she left. We've both had a really intense week.

I steal Ashley's binoculars so I can see every second. She only half protests until the gun goes off. Then she and everyone else around me starts screaming for Juniper. I wish I could see her face, but her back is toward me as she races down the water. Juniper is two lengths ahead of the field within a minute of shoving off. I can see the muscles of her back working, can tell she's clenching her jaw in concentration. *Relax, baby,* I think, and as if she heard me, I see her shoulders drop and her body tension eases. Now she's really flying down the water.

The beads of water off the end of her oars glisten like diamonds in the sunshine. Every person here is on their feet screaming for her. It's not even a race anymore, but an opportunity to see just how fast my girl can get here. I look at the judges, and they're all either grinning like fools or have their jaws dropped in shock. My girl is fast as fuck, and now everyone knows it.

A few strokes to go and she'll be here. I'm flying out of my seat and down the bleachers. I want mine to be the face Juniper sees when she crosses the line and pulls up her oars. I get as close to the water as I can. Bam! She's past. Her chest heaves as she pulls up and just leans back, gliding to a stop.

But then our eyes lock and we are the only people in the world. She makes her way to the dock to climb out of her boat, and I'm stumbling over to her. I crouch down and lift her out of the seat and into my arms. My lips crash into hers as she melts into my arms. This is all I want. Right here. This moment, this woman.

"You came to see my race," she whispers against my chest.

"Baby, you're going to have to do more than not tell me about it if you plan to keep me away." I start laughing and kiss her some more. I can never get enough of how she tastes, and the salty musk of her sweat just adds to her appeal for me right now. Finally, I pull back and cup her chin in my hand. "Juniper Jones, I love you," I say. I can't hold it in anymore. "I love you."

She starts crying then, which I was not expecting, but I also know how emotional I get when I'm competing. She buries her face in my chest and, with a muffled voice, she says, "I never thought I would have any of this."

"Any of what, JJ?"

She waves her hand around. "All of this. Love. Success. Rowing. Just all of it."

"Of course you have all these things, baby. You earned all these things." I'm starting to freak out a little that she hasn't said anything specifically about loving me back, when she bites my neck.

"I love you, Tyrion Stag." And then she kisses me, soft and tender, hungry and longing. Eventually I realize some of the cheering and wolf-whistling I hear is Ashley and Tina and the other rowers standing around waiting to congratulate Juniper. Guess the cat is out of the bag about us being together. *Good,* I think, and kiss her even harder.

Derrick has to peel Juniper out of my arms for the award ceremony and I cheer louder than anyone when they slip that medal around her neck. Some old codger takes the microphone and announces that Juniper's time was the fastest on record for that race length, and he's thrilled to offer her a spot on the women's national team. "I'll have you know I raced with your father in Montreal in 1976," he says, pumping her hand. "It will be my honor and my pleasure to serve on your coaching staff as we prepare for Tokyo next year."

When Juniper finishes hugging everyone and crying, I tug her over to my rental car. I've had about all I can stand of looking at her in spandex race gear. I need to get her naked, pronto.

She sits back in her seat, looking so content as I speed to my hotel. I park in a screech of tires. She squeaks when I jump out, pull her door open, and lift her out of the car. I toss her over one shoulder and she starts smacking my ass while I walk to my room. "Ty, put me down. People can see!"

"Baby, I don't give a shit who can see. I need you and I need you now."

I slide the key card into the slot and see the green light I've been waiting for. I stride over to the bed and ease Juniper onto it as I'm peeling off my shorts.

She shakes her head at me, laughing. "We don't have to hide anymore, baby," I say, stepping out of my boxers. I'm naked in front of her, and she's still fully dressed in her uniform.

"What do you mean we don't have to hide? What did you do?" She crawls back, like she's trying to get away from me.

"I talked to my brother and I told him I love you and you're not my lawyer anymore," I say, crawling onto the bed after her. My dick is so hard it's lying up against my stomach, and I see her look at it, licking those luscious lips of hers.

"I was going to talk to him on Monday," she whispers. When I finally reach her, I start licking the hollow of her throat, kissing her shoulder.

"Mmmhmm," I moan. "More kissing, less talking about my brother." This gets a giggle from her, and she starts to peel off her spandex tank top. I help her out with the little shorts and ease her down so she's lying back on the bed.

"Ty, I'm all sweaty and gross," she says, but doesn't really make an effort to move.

"You taste amazing," I say, licking the salty skin of one collarbone. Just thinking of her working so hard today, that determined look on her face, is enough to drive me wild with want.

I nestle in between her legs, tickling her stomach with the medal she left on. I brush the cool metal across a pert nipple, flicking the other one with my tongue until Juniper begins to moan. "I've missed you, baby," I say, dragging my tongue around each nipple while she starts to writhe beneath my chest. Her nipples feel so good against my skin.

She reaches down and finds my cock, and a groan escapes my

throat. Her hand feels so good wrapped around my shaft. I'm lost in the sensation and I don't fully notice what Juniper is doing until I realize she has me lined up against her hot entrance. Bare.

I raise an eyebrow at her, questioning.

She pulls me down by the shoulders. "I read those articles you sent me," she says, now licking my chest in all the ways I'd been licking her a few minutes ago. "I'm on the pill."

My animal brain takes over with those words, and I waste no time sinking inside her. "Holy fuck this feels good," I practically grunt. Her pussy is so wet, so tight and smooth against my skin. "Juniper!"

She wraps those long legs around me, her heels driving me deeper into her body, pressed into my ass cheeks. I'm about to lose control, but not before I get her there first. I brace myself on my forearms, angling my hips so my body rubs right up against her clit. I find the friction I know she needs when she drops her head back and starts screaming my name.

I fucking love how loud she is right now as I drive into her, nothing between us. Just me and Juniper Jones. I can feel it when her orgasm rips through her. She starts to spasm around my cock, her hips bucking wildly off the bed. "Fuck, baby, yes," I shout, and then I'm with her.

I feel it start to spiral inside me and then my balls draw up tight. My release fires inside of her again and again, thick ropes of ecstasy. My dick twitches and finally rests, and I collapse on top of my lady, both of us heaving and gasping for breath.

"Ty, that was amazing," she whispers.

"Mmm you're telling me," I say, tracing letters on her back as I pull her against my chest. "I'm never letting you go, you know."

She   nods.   "I'm   ok   with   that."

Epilogue: Ty

Tokyo, Summer Olympics

"Ty, baby, everyone here is flipping the fuck out," Matty yells into my cell. I'm about to hang up on him, but Juniper's race start is delayed for wind so I figure I'll let him blow off some steam. The Fury made it to the Stanley Cup playoffs again, and I'm missing a whole slew of television appearances and parades and shit, to be here with Juniper.

Matty is talking up a blue streak and eventually I cut him off. "Look, if you think I'm going to miss watching my girl compete in the Olympics you're crazy. Take it up with my lawyer." He gasps, inhaling for another tirade, but I hang up on him. Ben will sort it all out. So what if I have to pay a penalty. Being here for Juniper is worth way more than any bonus pay.

My phone rings again, and I see it's my sister-in-law. "Hey, Alice, what's up?" I can hear the baby crying in the background and it sounds like she's pacing and trying to shush him to get him to calm down.

"Tim said it looks like Juniper's race is delayed. Just wondering if you knew how long? It's past bedtime here, but we all stayed up…"

"It looks like they're getting everything set up. I think the wind died down."

I can hear my brother shout in the background. "Did he say it's soon?"

"Yes, Timber, it's soon!" I shout so loud that the other husbands and boyfriends all turn around to look at me. "Ok, fam, I gotta go. The Dutch are annoyed that I'm on the phone." I roll my eyes and slide my phone into my pocket. I'm ready to behave, until the race starts anyway.

I try to sit calmly. Juniper has trained so hard for this moment. Everything at work is so rewarding for her now that she won all sorts of money and regulations for the women hockey players, and I got the Fury to all pose for some solidarity promo shots with their team. It's been pretty amazing.

But Juniper is so disciplined with her sport, too. For me, the best thing about her training is how it helps me with my own game. I moved out of my grandma's house soon after Juniper and I went public with our relationship. We got a bigger townhouse together, near where her old one was, so she would still be close enough to the boathouse to row before work.

It's easy to keep up a good diet and conditioning routine when you're doing it with the person you love and live with. She even comes to the weight room with me sometimes. Derrick might be sleeping with one of my trainers, but I'm not entirely sure. Anyway, Juniper and I are both fit as hell and peaking at just the right time. We push each other to be better. I need her, and I want to be there for her in every way she needs me.

A hush rolls over the crowd as the race finally gets started. It's a long course and there's no way to see the start from here, so they've got the race broadcasted on a giant screen. I know this won't be another New Haven where Juniper wins by like five boat lengths. These women are the best in the world, but they've never raced my Junebug. I wish her father could see her now as she sits at the start line, face determined. The camera zooms in on her in her USA gear and my heart swells with pride.

I hear the gun and I hear the crowd around me, but I don't look away from Juniper on the monitor. The camera stays close with her, because she holds the lead from the very beginning. I can see the French boat creeping up on her, and I start to scream for her to dig deep, even though she is too far away to hear me. And dig she does. Juniper Jones comes into view almost a full length ahead of her next competitors.

When she finally glides across the finish, I can see all the happiness in the world streaming from her face with her tears. My girl just won an Olympic gold medal.

"Yes!" I jump in the air and start trying to give high fives to my European seat mates, who must not celebrate that way because they have no idea what I'm doing.

I start to climb down the bleachers and make my way toward Juniper. I know in my heart I'm going to marry this woman. I'm not going to ask her today, though. This is about her. About her victory, her moment. I'm here to support her.

She finds me up in the crowd and we make our way toward each other. She lays a kiss on me that just about knocks me back, and I know there's no other place in the world I'd rather be than right here with her.

~~~

Want more Ty and Juniper?
Click here for a steamy bonus scene:
BookHip.com/XQQSJT

Can't get enough Stag Brothers?
Thatcher's story continues in Fragile Illusion!

Made in the USA
Monee, IL
13 March 2023